Catherine's Son

Catherine's Son

The Story of a Boy
Who Became an Outlaw

James L. Smith

Suncrest Publications
Las Cruces, NM

Suncrest Publications
Las Cruces, NM

Cover Art
Copyright © 2012 by Emma Henderson
www.emmamema.com

ISBN-13: 978-0-9701589-4-9
LCCN: 2012953050

1 3 5 7 9 8 6 4 2

For
Mark and Christopher

Author's Note

This book is a work of fiction. It deals with the time when Henry McCarty, a boy known to history as Billy the Kid, lived with his mother in Silver City, a mining camp in the New Mexico Territory. Little is known about most of Billy the Kid's short life, especially the time he lived in Silver City, and fiction is sometimes the only way to fill the gaps in his story. Although the significant characters and events in this book are real, the author acknowledges that the tale is told with an unconventional perspective on Billy the Kid. If it adds to the Kid's myth, so be it. His timeless legend is dynamic enough for another version of how he became an outlaw.

New York City
July 1863

Prologue

Catherine McCarty received a letter in early July informing her that her husband Michael had died. The letter came from a soldier named Patrick Fitzgerald and had taken six months to arrive. The last letter she had received from Michael had been written before Christmas, and she had assumed he was still serving under General Rosecrans in Tennessee. The letter from Private Fitzgerald contained little information about Michael's death, stating only that he had been killed at Stones River. His passing had been quick and painless, wrote Private Fitzgerald.

Before Michael left New York to fight for the Union, he had promised Catherine that when he returned he would take her and their two boys out of the Bowery. She had told him often that she wanted to leave. The gangs of young men roaming the streets frightened her, and she worried about what might happen to her children as they got older. Billy was not yet four, Josie was a baby, and she did not want them growing up surrounded by the wickedness she saw every day.

Now that Michael was gone, she was on her own to decide where to raise her boys, and when the riots broke out two weeks after she learned of Michael's death, she knew more than ever that she needed to leave the city.

The lawlessness that spread through New York that July began shortly after people filled the streets to protest the government's conscription policies. Republicans had not only been drafting men unwilling to fight for the Union, they had been allowing draftees from wealthy families to hire substitutes or pay deferment fees. The young men who lived in the slums called the war a "poor man's fight," and they were determined to let federal agents know they would not cooperate with any law forcing them to serve the Union cause.

Catherine understood their anger. The conscription policy *was* unfair. What Catherine didn't understand was how easily the protests turned into an assault on people who had done no harm. In only a few hours, a demonstration against government policy had reshaped itself into the fury of a ferocious mob intent on killing all federal agents. The mob's savage attacks then deteriorated into a desire to exterminate the people believed to be most responsible for the war — people of color.

Catherine had long known that the gangs of young men in her neighborhood were capable of hurting each other, but she had never thought their everyday unruliness could so easily degenerate into a massacre of innocent people. She had never before seen anyone die violently, and that summer, during the riots, she watched a bloodthirsty mob kill three people.

The first was a colored man who worked as a meat cutter in a shop located only a short walk from where she lived. She had heard customers at the shop call him Ellard, and she had often purchased meat from him. She did not know the woman and little girl who were with him when he died, but assumed they were his wife and daughter. The girl looked no more than three, the same age as Billy.

Catherine never understood why Ellard and his family were walking through her neighborhood that evening, especially in the midst of a riot. They might have been heading home from his work at the butcher shop. They might also have been lost in the chaos of a city set on fire. Whatever the reason, Catherine could not help but notice how frightened they looked, walking close to each other, holding hands, trying to remain unseen in the shadows of the tenements.

At first, the smoke twisting down the street had kept them hidden from the rioters, but the fires spreading through the neighborhood that night made their safe escape impossible. The streets glowed with a hazy orange light that cut through the smoke and exposed them to a mob of Irish ruffians. When the hooligans caught sight of a colored family in their midst, they dashed toward them with clubs and a diseased prejudice.

Catherine watched a dozen men grab the woman and her daughter and shove them into the street. She then watched several others attack Ellard pulling him to the ground and taking the worn-out shoes off his feet before stripping him of his yellow waistcoat and coffee-colored shirt. After his white linen trousers were pulled away, he was left naked on the ground. The mob then beat him without mercy before lifting him to his feet and dragging him up a flight of stairs attached to the outside wall of a tenement house. At the top of the stairs they placed a rope around his neck.

Catherine knew at once that the terror in Ellard's eyes would haunt her forever. He stood motionless, and his ghostly stare brought her to tears. She then watched in horror as two men pushed him from the balcony. The noose girdling his throat snapped his neck and jerked his body up from its fall, leaving his corpse swinging mother-naked in the night air.

Having already seen too much, Catherine turned away, only to see a crowd of people gathered around her, standing on their toes, stretching their necks to gawk at what had happened. Above the crowd's cheers and laughter, Catherine heard the anguished screams of Ellard's wife and daughter. She wanted to help them, but there was nothing she could do. She could neither bring back the man they loved nor protect them from the mob that also wanted to kill them.

Catherine had tried to keep Billy and Josie away from the madness, but failed. She had wanted to keep them safe inside the tenement where she lived and out of the street where innocent people were dying, but she abandoned that plan after a fire set by rioters spread through her neighborhood. Smoke filled the corridors of the tenement house, and she had no choice but to take her boys outside.

Josie was too young to know what was happening. Billy, however, was old enough to be frightened by what he saw. Catherine would have prevented him from watching the lynching, but she was carrying Josie in her arms and could not free her hands to cover Billy's eyes. She then had no time to whisk him away from what happened after the lynching.

With Ellard hanging dead at the end of a rope, the mob turned its rage on his wife and daughter, beating them both with unrestrained fury. Catherine felt Billy's tiny body tremble next to her as his innocent eyes, wide as Belleek saucers, watched the woman and her child die in front of him. Catherine stood powerless as the blood of the dying mother and daughter rippled beneath her son's feet. One of the men clubbing the little girl looked directly into Billy's eyes and hissed the word "justice" before spitting on the girl's corpse.

Federal troops occupied New York several days later and ended the rioting. But even with the city at peace, Catherine was determined to take her boys out of the Bowery. The longer she stayed, the greater the chance they might grow into the type of young men she had seen murdering Ellard and his family, men made so irrational by the frustration of their lives that they were willing to do the devil's work.

It was the mission of Catherine's life to raise her boys well, and she wanted to find a place where they could grow up and become good men. She wanted to tell them stories of honorable people, and she did not want those stories tarnished by the brutality of people they knew in their own lives.

She had no money to return to Ireland, to the beautiful Lough Neagh where she had once lived, and she decided to move west to the land that seemed full of opportunities for her and her boys. She understood that she would be taking Billy and Josie into unfamiliar and rugged territory, but she hoped they would do well as long as they were guided by a mother who wanted only the best for them, a mother who wanted them to know every day that she loved them, a mother who wanted to keep their young souls unspoiled by the injustices of this world.

There was a big crowd gazing at me wasn't there? Well, perhaps some of them will think me half man now; everyone seems to think I am some kind of an animal.

  – Henry McCarty, alias Billy the Kid, sitting in a jail cell, his arms and legs shackled, seven months before he was shot dead at age twenty-one

Silver City, New Mexico Territory
September 1873

Henry McCarty would not remain a victim. He may have been nothing more than a scrawny thirteen-year-old boy, wearing the tattered clothes his nine-year-old brother had outgrown, but he would make sure the other boys in town respected him. Some of them had made fun at his expense, guying him for being so small. Even his mother sometimes worried he was too little to take care of himself, but she had no reason to be concerned. This would be the night he would do something to end the teasing of at least one of the boys.

Chauncey Truesdell had been ridiculing him without mercy, calling him a sissy, a milksop, a mama's boy. At first, Henry tried not to make issue of the name calling, flashing a wide grin to ward off Chauncey's insults. But when Chauncey placed a dog turd on his chair at the dance hall, he couldn't let it pass. It was time to get even. Better to be an offender than a victim, he figured.

With his pal Louis Abraham beside him, Henry stood outside the Truesdells' red brick home. He was far enough from Main Street and the center of the town's hustle and bustle that he had little fear of getting caught. The sun had set over the silver mines west of town, and he had calculated that it was too dark for Chauncey's mother to catch sight of what he and Louis were getting ready to do. Not only was it growing dark, but an outdoor privy stood between him and the window of the Truesdells' parlor. He knew Mrs. Truesdell was sitting in the parlor because he couldn't see her through the windows of any other rooms. Mr. Truesdell would be no problem because he had left town several days earlier on a mail run. Chauncey, meanwhile, sat in the privy in front of Henry, unaware that Henry was preparing to have a little fun at his expense.

Henry reached into his vest pocket to grab a strip of yellow paper covered with Chinese characters. He unwrapped the paper, exposing a dozen Lucifer matches he had purchased that morning from Charlie Sun. If the first Lucifer didn't ignite, he would still have extras to set fire to the cloth bag he had already stuffed with cottonwood chips and soaked in kerosene.

"This should loosen his bowels," Henry whispered to Louis. He struck one of the matches on a small stone. Louis, holding the bag at arm's length, waited for Henry to set it on fire.

Henry's plan could not have gone better. After he set fire to the bag, Louis dropped it through an opening at the bottom of the outhouse. Chauncey had been inside the outhouse for at least five minutes before the bag was dropped, and when the small structure filled with smoke, Henry knew Chauncey would soon be coming out. Henry heard Chauncey bumping against the door and struggling with the latch. Chauncey finally pushed the door open, only to fall outside, his pants cuffing his ankles. As he lifted himself to his knees, Henry splashed him with bucket of horse piss that he had carried all the way from the Legal Tender Corral. Unlike the matches that had cost him a penny, he had paid nothing for the horse piss, telling Mr. Hudson he needed it for keeping the cats away from his mother's garden. After the piss smacked Chauncey in the face, Henry watched Chauncey spit and sputter, looking as if he had just stuck his nose into the wrong end of a skunk.

"Just paying you what I owe you," Henry said, his buckteeth exaggerating the grin on his face.

While Chauncey reached down to pull up his pants, Henry yanked Louis's arm and pulled him out of the Truesdells' yard. The boys then began running as fast as their calfskin moccasins could carry them. As they moved down the hill toward town, Louis ran a step behind Henry, his laughter robbing him of the breath he needed to keep up with his friend.

"Don't fall too far behind," Henry said, also laughing, "or Chauncey'll beat on you till you're blue."

Chauncey was nowhere in sight and must have been still buttoning his pants by the time Henry and Louis reached the bottom of the hill. When they got to Main Street they turned to see if Chauncey had caught up with them. They were standing outside Mr. Bailey's apothecary. Across the street Henry could see light shining from the window of the cabin where he lived.

They waited no more than a couple of minutes before the piss-soaked Chauncey emerged from the darkness. Chauncey stood alone, more than a block away, silhouetted against a fire glowing through the window of an adobe home. Henry watched Chauncey punching the air with his fists in anger and frustration. Henry knew that the winning cards were now on his side of the table.

"I'll owe you a favor for helping me," Henry said to Louis,

feeling satisfied that he'd finally pulled a notch ahead of Chauncey.

"We've certainly given him reason to quit treating you like you're not worth a tinker's damn," Louis said.

"I hope so," Henry said, smiling. "I'd just as soon be that boy's friend and not someone throwing horse piss in his face."

— 2 —

After Henry walked into his family's cabin, he found his mother reading from the light cast by a kerosene lamp placed next to her on the table. He had been told that he looked like her, that his light brown hair and powder blue eyes were the same as hers. More than once he had heard that no one would ever doubt he was Catherine Antrim's son.

Still breathing hard from the sprint down the hill to get away from Chauncey, he stepped behind his mother and peered over her shoulder. She was looking at an obituary in *Mining Life*, the town's weekly gazette.

"Anyone we know?" he asked.

She reached behind her to pat his cheek. "A man was stabbed at the Orleans Club. They don't know his name. It appears Silver City is just another town with too many barroom brawls and too much redeye whiskey. The saloons here seem to be as wild as those we left behind in Wichita and Denver."

"What about the ones in Santa Fe?" Henry asked.

"We didn't live there long enough to form an opinion, did we?"

Even though Catherine had left Ireland long before Henry was born, she had never lost the accent that marked her as a immigrant.

"At least what's happening in the saloons is not as bad as dealing with the Apache," Henry said. "Harry Whitehill's father told me that only two years ago he wondered if the town would ever be safe from their attacks."

"By our good fortune that problem calmed down before we arrived. I hear that a few good people sacrificed their lives to protect this town, and except for what's going on in the saloons, I've been told this place is safer than what it was two years ago. But I still don't want you traveling alone on the roads leaving town. I didn't bring you here to get ambushed by renegades — whether they're Indians or Christians."

Henry leaned forward to see more of the newspaper and caught the familiar smell of lavender. His mother held a pouch of dried lavender buds in her left hand. She had purchased the pouch at a store in Wichita and brought it all the way to Silver City in a pocket sewn on the front of her dress. She often took a whiff, although its aroma was not as strong as it had once been.

No more than ten feet away, Henry's little brother Josie sat on an old packing crate, gazing out a small window next to the fireplace. As usual, he just sat, doing nothing.

Henry looked at his brother's stone-faced expression and wondered what he was thinking about, if he was even thinking. Josie was four years younger than Henry. Even so, he was taller and more solidly built. Josie might be bigger, Henry had often thought, but he's certainly not smarter.

Henry found it difficult to talk with his brother. Books were scattered around the cramped cabin, but Josie couldn't discuss what was in the books because he never bothered reading them. He also couldn't talk about the events of his day because he rarely left the cabin. On occasion, he whittled on a piece of cottonwood root, and if anyone asked what he was making, he would reply with a shrug, "Nothing, just whittling."

"Where have you been?" Catherine asked, turning to look at Henry.

"I finally pulled even with Chauncey. He had pushed me too far, and I played a joke on him."

Catherine tweaked her son's cheek and smiled.

"I've been hoping you would stand up to that boy. I've heard him hound you when he's around the cabin."

Henry had expected his mother to take his side. She usually did.

"What did you do to him?" she asked. "I hope you didn't hurt him. His mother is a good friend of mine."

Henry recounted the story of the smoking outhouse, changing only one little detail. He told his mother that he had thrown a bucket of water in Chauncey's face, rather than horse piss. He knew that she would not have approved of that part of the story. She would have preferred that he had saved the horse piss to keep the cats out of the garden.

Catherine was forty-three years old, a shadow of the high-spirited beauty that Henry figured she had once been. Her walnut-colored hair, hanging loose under a blue scarf, radiated a healthy shine that offset the pale skin and dark circles under her eyes. Her eyes nevertheless sparkled, especially when she laughed, and the story of what Henry had done to Chauncey made her laugh.

"Where's Bill?" Henry asked.

"Gone, as usual," Josie said, breaking into the conversation.

"He who is alive speaks!" Henry said, mocking Josie's high-pitched voice.

Catherine shook her finger at Henry. "I see no need to tease your brother."

Henry rolled his eyes and offered a halfhearted apology.

"Bill's gone prospecting," Catherine said. "He told me he'll be back in a few days."

More like a few weeks, Henry thought. As far as Henry was concerned, his stepfather was a pie-eyed son-of-a-bitch, and the family was better off without him. The red-bearded bastard's story was always the same. He would leave town, telling everyone he was seeking his family's fortune. He would then come home several days, sometimes weeks, later, penniless and drunk. Henry never knew where Bill went or what he did when he was gone. Henry did know that his family had no fortune. His mother kept everything afloat with little help from her husband.

The son-of-a-bitch had also stolen Henry's name, the name given to him when he was born. Henry had been christened William Henry McCarty, and people had always called him Billy, a name he liked, but his stepfather wouldn't let him keep that name.

"Two Billys in one family is confusing," Bill had told Henry on the day he married Henry's mother. "We'll call you by your middle name."

Henry never understood the logic. Bill Antrim was a grown man and people no longer called him Billy. Henry figured most people could tell the difference between a *man* named Bill and a *boy* named Billy. To hell with those who couldn't.

His mother had asked him not to make issue of his stepfather's request. "When you're old enough, you can stake claim to any name you want," she had said. "In the meantime, be grateful for your family name. People will always know you as a McCarty, not an Antrim."

Henry went along. If his mother wanted it, he wouldn't go against her. He'd wait until he was older and then reclaim the name given to him at birth. Until then, he'd hold tight to the name McCarty, the name of his real father, the name he carried with pride.

— 3 —

Henry and his family lived in a cramped one-room log cabin. A bed, a table, and a Franklin stove took up most of the space, giving Henry plenty of reason to stay outside playing with his friends.

"This place is too small to swing a cat," he had told his mother when they first moved in.

The cabin was not as roomy as the three-room, balloon-framed house where they had lived in Wichita, and it didn't compare favorably to some of the eastern-looking brick homes owned by the wealthier families in town. Henry's mother had told him not to complain. "We're better off than most," she had said. "Walk around Silver City and look at how most of the miners are living. You'll be thankful for what we've got."

The silver deposits west of town and the stamp mills south of town had caused people as far away as Denver to talk about Silver City as the treasure vault of the New Mexico Territory. After news spread that 300 tons of ore had been extracted in less than two years, people were saying the town was a prospector's paradise. The town was less than three years old and a thousand people had already moved in. Most of the people — primarily miners from Britain and Mexico — lived in canvas tents, and after seeing how much rain could fall in town during the late summer, Henry agreed with his mother that a one-room log cabin, although small, wasn't as bad as the tents where the miners were sleeping.

Henry and Josie had helped their mother and stepfather turn the cabin into a suitable home. They had made a table out of old boards and nailed packing crates to the squared-log walls to serve as cabinets. They helped Bill install a pinewood floor, repair leaks in the roof, and fill cracks between the logs. They planted fruit trees outside and scrubbed the stone fireplace clean inside, giving their mother the means of baking sweetcakes in the firebox. Henry had even crawled up the chimney to brush soot out of the flue.

"That fireplace and that Franklin will bring us an income," Catherine had told Henry. "We'll bake pastries and sell them in front of the cabin."

Henry, on his own, had pieced together scraps of ticking cloth and stuffed them with straw to place on the floor next to the fireplace. When the weather turned cold he and Josie would then have a warm place to sleep. Until then, on the nights that it wasn't raining, they dragged their straw pallets outside and slept under the cottonwood trees growing next to the cabin.

On the September evening that Henry had soaked Chauncey with horse piss, he and Josie would not be able to sleep under the cottonwoods. Clouds had moved over the town, covering the stars and dropping the temperature lower than it had been since April. When thunder began to shake the cabin, Catherine asked Henry and Josie to come inside.

"Into each life some rain will fall," she told them as they dragged their pallets through the door. "There will always be days that are dark and dreary."

Henry figured the cloudburst and the light rain that followed would drop enough water to flood the spot next to the trees where he usually slept. By morning, Main Street, which ran in front of the cabin, would probably be drenched and impassable.

Even though he was dry inside the cabin, Henry couldn't get to sleep that night and remained awake long after the cloudburst had ended and the thunder died down. Wedged uncomfortably between his brother and the foundation of the fireplace, which was made of sharp stone, he entertained himself by thinking about what he had just done to Chauncey. If Chauncey's taunts continued, Henry would next time place a snake in the privy. It was always good to think ahead, he figured.

He eventually grew tired of thinking about Chauncey and turned his attention toward the soothing rhythm of the drizzling rain dropping on the cabin's gabled roof. Unable to make himself comfortable, he stuck his elbow into Josie's ribs, hoping to make his brother roll over, but Josie didn't respond. Finally, late into the night, he fell asleep with the gentle sound of falling water calming his thoughts.

Before he had time to begin dreaming, he was awakened by the familiar sound of his mother coughing and gasping for air. What he heard was the most recognizable symptom of an illness that had plagued her for years. She called it the "bloody dog" — her name for the barking cough and the bloody phlegm that it produced. It was the bloody dog that had brought Henry and his family to Silver City.

In Wichita, Catherine had run a laundry that was so profitable she was able to buy a home on the edge of town and purchase additional plots of land within town. She had attended community council meetings, becoming the only woman to sign a petition calling for the town's incorporation. If she had not grown ill she would have never left Wichita — but that was not the case. The bloody dog was deciding her fate.

Doctors said she had tuberculosis. Some people called it consumption. By any name, Henry couldn't help but notice that the illness had stolen her energy and sapped her spirit. She was no longer the vibrant woman who once owned her own laundry. Some days she was too exhausted even to get out of bed.

Henry had heard some people say the disease was a punishment for moral shortcomings, claiming people who had it weren't good Christians. Henry knew that was nonsense. His mother was as good a person as he knew.

"The doctor can't explain what caused me to get sick," she had told Henry. "He said it might have been the heat and steam from the laundry."

Whatever the cause, Henry wished the disease would go away.

"They've set up sanatoriums in Europe for what I have," she had told him, "but we're not so advanced over here. The only advice I get from the doctor is to find a dry climate." That advice prompted her to leave Wichita and move to the New Mexico Territory.

At first, Henry thought Silver City's climate had helped her. During the late spring and early summer, her coughing had disappeared. She had seemed stronger and less tired, more apt to spend time baking sweetcakes and visiting friends. Henry had even heard her say she might open another laundry in Silver City. But when the late summer rains placed too much moisture in the air, her hacking, resonant cough returned, ending her talk of another laundry.

Henry had learned that when the bloody dog attacked, Bill and

Josie were of no use. If Bill was home, which was rare, the coughing attacks simply made him leave the cabin. It was obvious to Henry that Bill preferred nursing a few shots of *aguardiente* in a high-spirited saloon rather than taking care of a sick woman in a claustrophobic cabin, even if that woman was his wife. More than once, Henry had watched Bill abandon Catherine right in the middle of an attack, cursing her as he left the cabin.

"I married a goddamned lunger," he would say. "Might as well get something to drink. I certainly can't get any sleep." He would then slam the door behind him as he left.

Josie usually slept through the bouts of coughing — or at least pretended to sleep. During the day, when he was awake, he seemed unconcerned about his mother's illness and indifferent to her needs.

Henry never understood how Bill and Josie could look the other away when someone they should have loved was so sick. She needed help. At the very least, she needed someone to hold a towel and catch the blood and sputum that accompanied her desperate attempts to breathe. With no one else willing to help her, Henry had long been her caretaker, the one who spent endless nights sitting next to her as she struggled with the bloody dog.

On this September night, her congested breathing served as a dissonant counterpoint to the sound of water dripping from the roof. As the rain fell, Henry helped her sit up. "I'll hold the towel," he said. "Let the bloody dog do its business. It'll soon go away."

Catherine spit mucus and blood of such volume that Henry feared he would need more towels. If he ran out, he was prepared to use his one extra shirt to catch her blood.

"Coughs and love don't hide easily," he said to his mother, repeating the words she had once used to comfort him when he was sick.

She looked up with swollen eyes and smiled. "Can you pour me a glass of water?" she asked, her voice faint and raspy from coughing.

Henry saw that the water bucket next to the table was empty. "I'll have to go outside."

"Don't go out in the rain," she pleaded. "If I have to wait until morning, I won't be any sicker than I am now."

Henry ignored her request and put on his moccasins to walk outside and gather water from the cistern behind the cabin. As rain soaked his clothes, he listened to the ragged sound of his mother's cough piercing the night air. He dipped a bucket into the barrel and wondered whether she would be able to survive the illness. Its reappearance made him doubt that the move to Silver City had been worthwhile.

Her cough worsened after he returned to the cabin. "Hold on till morning," he said. "You know it's not as bad during the day." He stroked her forehead with a wet cloth and told her, "Make it through the night and tomorrow you'll feel better. You might even feel strong enough to go to McGary's. I've never known you to be too sick to dance the polka or schottische."

She smiled at him and nodded in agreement. "I would love to go to dancing," she said.

— 4 —

The next evening Henry escorted his mother to the dance hall at McGary's. He moved unhurried down the street, making sure that when his mother arrived she would still have enough energy to keep up with the music.

With no dry walkways in front of the newer buildings, Henry and his mother were forced to sidestep the puddles left over from the previous night's rain. As they walked, Henry took note of the familiar smell he associated with Main Street, a smell that combined the odor of raw sewage and burning pinewood. He also took note of the red brick buildings that were beginning to give Silver City a look of permanence. The town may have been nothing more than a three-year-old mining camp. But, as Henry had overheard one businessman say, "Silver City could become the Denver of the New Mexico Territory."

What Henry had never heard from any of the businessmen was a desire to take some of the money spent on red bricks and put it into making Chihuahua Hill more livable. Chihuahua Hill was a rocky slope rising from the south end of town that contained a Spanish-speaking community of people living in wood and adobe shacks. At night, as he slept under the cottonwoods next to the cabin, he enjoyed looking at the palette of lights illuminating the Hill. Even more, he enjoyed listening to the music and whoops of joy coming from the Hill's cantinas.

Henry's thoughts were pulled away from the red brick sturdiness of Main Street and the shoddy shacks on the Hill when his mother began talking about the rat's nest of saloons lining Main Street in front of them. Silver City had far more than its share of smoke-filled whiskey mills. Establishments such as the Blue Goose, the Blue Onion, and the Tiger never lacked patrons and stayed open late into the night. Joe Dyer's Orleans Club, with its regal decorations in the barroom and opium den in the back, ranked as the most popular — and violent — of the saloons.

"That's the cock-a-doodle-doo of democracy," Catherine said, pointing at the Orleans Club. "I want you to stay out of that place." Her Irish accent became more noticeable to Henry as she lectured him about the evils of saloons. "There's no profit in rubbing shoulders with the dregs that Mr. Dyer caters to. Only last month Mr. Dyer himself was stabbed in the stomach and his face was sliced open. He will be scarred for the rest of his life. He'll never be able to hide the markings of what he does for a living."

Henry's mother had spoken so many times about the type of man she wanted him to become that he could predict what she would say next. She would tell him to avoid hard liquor, letting him know that whiskey did little more than unleash the cruelty in men. She would say that she wanted him to stand up for himself and not let others force him to do something he knew he shouldn't do. She wanted him to fight for those who couldn't fight for themselves and always live his life on the side of the angels. He had heard it a hundred times, and he heard it again during that night's walk to McGary's.

"I took you and Josie out of the Bowery to get you away from the delinquents and derelicts who lived there," she said. "I don't plan on watching you befriend those type of men in this town."

"There's no need to worry," Henry said, laughing away her concerns. "Josie's too lazy to get into trouble, and I'm too likable. I have no desire to drink any of that redeye, and I'm not out to hurt anyone. Trust me, Mam, you raised a good boy." He knew how to ease his mother's fears.

"I know you're a good boy," she said, placing her hand in the angle of his arm and pulling him close. "I know you are."

Henry escorted his mother away from the batwing doors at the front of McGary's to the rear of the building. The front entrance was reserved for men who wanted to drink and gamble, which was a sizable number, to say the least. Silver City, after all, was well populated with the saloonkeepers and whores who made their living by serving migrants of the frontier.

But the town was also full of men and women who had brought their children with them, people who said they wanted to build a peaceful, law-abiding community that would endure for many years. For those types of people, William McGary had set aside a large room at the back of his saloon for events that would meet any mother's approval. Church services and sessions of district court were held there, and four nights a week McGary sponsored dances that catered to families. It was the double barn doors at the rear of McGary's that welcomed families onto a spacious dance floor.

William McGary had established strict rules of behavior for the dance hall. He allowed no cussing or fighting, and anyone who carried a bottle of whiskey into the place was thrown out. Silver City may have been home to the same riffraff as any other mining camp, but the dance hall had put William McGary on the side of high-minded people who wanted to build a civilized town. McGary wanted to do his part to make Silver City a suitable place for women and children.

Henry and his mother walked into the dance hall just as the music began to play. People were already moving onto the dance floor for the first two-stepping of the evening. In the far corner of the room a man played a scratched upright piano that sounded out of tune. Henry had heard the piano came to Silver City on the back of a mule, a journey that supposedly damaged it beyond repair. To Henry, the damages made no difference, as the piano always sounded good enough for dancing.

Unlike most evenings, when only the piano provided the music, McGary on this night had hired extra musicians. A fiddler and banjo player stood next to the piano.

"The music will be grand this evening," Henry said, as he spotted the three musicians. "I hope the fiddler will play *Turkey in the Straw*."

"He might if you ask him politely," Catherine said. "Good manners will usually get you what you want."

The dance hall was packed with people, and Henry enjoyed following his mother as she walked through the crowd. She was wearing her favorite dress, the one made of amaranth-colored cotton with a high collar and white lace trim on the sleeves. She greeted everyone — friend or stranger — with laughter and a gift for making them feel important. As always, her blue eyes locked onto the eyes of anyone talking to her, letting them know that what they were saying was the only thing important to her at that moment. She laughed at the jokes others told, and she made her own stories more humorous by embellishing them with her Irish accent.

After Henry had given his mother enough time to socialize, he was ready to dance and walked across the room to request a tune from the musicians. He asked if they could play *Turkey in the Straw*, and when they began playing it, he returned to his mother.

"Did you call for that song?" she asked.

Henry put his hands to his side and bowed at the waist. "Yes, and it's my desire that Katie McCarty dance with me."

"I'm always willing to dance with such a fine young gentleman as Billy McCarty."

Henry took his mother's hand and led her onto the dance floor. The smile on her face delighted him as she moved her feet to the music. Considering what the bloody dog had done to her the night before, he was relieved to see that she still had enough energy to have a good time.

After the final chord of the tune, Henry applauded with the rest of the crowd and then watched the musicians discuss what they would play next. The triple time of the piano player's introduction prepared them for a waltz — Catherine's favorite type of dance.

Henry began to three-step with his mother as the piano player accented the melody with left-hand chords on the second and third beats. The fiddler countered the piano's melody with triplets.

The banjo player, a fellow the fiddler had introduced to the crowd earlier as Sombrero Jack, hid his eyes under a turquoise and gold sombrero pulled low over his forehead. Standing motionless, he let his banjo remain silent for several bars before providing the dancers a musical entrance that revealed an embarrassing lack of talent. Henry wondered if maybe he'd just been drinking too much.

Henry could not figure out what Sombrero Jack was playing. Earlier, during *Turkey in the Straw*, the piano player and fiddler must have been drowning out his inept musicianship. But the waltz exposed the clumsiness of his playing. He sounded like he was performing Chinese music to accompany an Irish three-step, and it wasn't long before his improvisations forced the fiddler to quit playing.

Henry was not alone in his failed attempts to find the beat. His mother kept stopping and listening for the right moment to get moving again. Some people left the dance floor, while others were unwilling to surrender to the confusion. Henry watched as they moved their bodies to a beat that was being sabotaged by a musician who desperately needed to practice his instrument.

"I think they're trying to play *Cream City Waltz*," Henry said.

"He's trying his best," Catherine said. "But trying doesn't make the music sweet. The way he's making people stumble and stagger, we're going to need a new name for this dance."

When the tune finally ended, Sombrero Jack was rewarded with laughter and a few jeers. He stood silently, accepting the crowd's response, grinning smugly under the sombrero that covered his eyes. To Henry, he looked pleased that his performance had generated so much laughter.

"Only fools laugh when others are laughing at them," Catherine whispered to Henry.

Sombrero Jack leaned his banjo against the wall and waved to the crowd as he left the dance hall. The piano player and fiddler, no doubt glad that Jack was gone, continued the music with a tune named *Bonnie Little Belle*. Henry wasted no time getting his mother started on the lively step-step-step-hop of the schottische.

He watched his mother's feet bounce with energy and noticed that she looked much younger than her forty-three years. Her illness may have knocked her down a few times, but the music at McGary's always got her moving again. She began to sing as she danced, bringing a smile to Henry's face. He couldn't help but sing along.

— 5 —

Just as the piano player and fiddler finished playing *Bonnie Little Belle*, Henry spotted Louis Abraham entering the dance hall with his sister Sarah. They were escorted by their father David, the owner of a local dry goods store and one of the wealthiest men in town.

Henry was pleased to see Louis come to McGary's. Louis was his friend, as well as his best opportunity to spend time with Sarah. Sarah was the one girl in town that Henry liked more than any other. She was the same age as him and seemed to like him as much as he liked her. She was kind and intelligent, and her delicate good looks were out of place in a town like Silver City. On this night, her blond hair was tied behind her head rather than hanging loose, the way she usually wore it. She was wearing a floor-length calico dress that Henry had never seen.

"Will you be okay if I leave you alone and visit with Louis and Sarah for a moment?" Henry asked his mother.

"Three dances in a row, and I admit I need a rest. Give me time to drink tea and visit with Mary Hudson, and we'll dance again later."

"I'll be ready." Henry then left his mother to talk with Louis and Sarah.

He was eager to start a conversation with Sarah, but first had to endure listening to Louis tell the latest news about Chauncey. "I hear he plans to get even with us," Louis said.

"That's to be expected," Henry said. "But there's no need to worry. We'll do something to him before he can do something to us. I've been thinking about putting a garden snake in his outhouse."

Before he could elaborate, he looked to the side and caught sight of Chauncey walking into the dance hall with his mother. Henry felt his jaw tighten. He hoped the confrontation he was getting ready to have with Chauncey would not involve Mrs.

Truesdell. He liked Mrs. Truesdell. She was his mother's good friend.

Henry was about to tell Louis that Chauncey was in the room, but before he could say anything he found that Louis must have already seen Chauncey. Louis had fled and left him alone. He then spotted Louis walking toward the dance floor with his sister, no doubt to avoid a confrontation with Chauncey.

Chauncey, meanwhile, was already charging across the room toward Henry. "I need to see you outside," Chauncey said, poking Henry in the chest.

"I'm ready." Henry said, poking Chauncey in return. Henry did not intend to back away, even though Chauncey was taller and heavier.

The two boys left through the barn doors at the rear of McGary's and walked into the shadows of the alley next to the Keystone Hotel.

"That burning bag left such a bad smell in our privy that my mother had to do her business at the Hudson's today." Chauncey's face was turning red. "My father's coming home tomorrow, and he's not going to like what you did. He'll blame me."

"Holy shit and shove me in it. I don't feel sorry for you. You had it coming. I have no regrets about what I did."

Chauncey clenched his fist. "What's wrong with you? Pulling a trick like that. Hitting me with a stinky bucket of piss."

"I don't appreciate the name calling, and I sure don't like sitting in dog shit."

"Is that what this is about? You can't take a joke?"

"If you can spoon it out, you should be able to take it."

Henry was determined to stand his ground. He wanted

29

Chauncey to show him the same respect a once-bit dog would show a rattlesnake.

"Let's make a deal," Chauncey said. "I'll end the name calling, if you'll promise no more pranks."

"Why so quick to back down? I was expecting you to fight, not surrender."

"I just don't want any more childish japes getting me in trouble. My mother's not happy about what happened, and my father's not going to like it when he finds out what you did to our privy."

"Why should I care?"

"I better be able to tell my mother and father that your jokes are done. If not, I'll get whipped until I can't sit down. They're going to blame me for your mischief."

"They'd be right."

"Let's end it now. No more insults. No more pranks." Chauncey was almost begging.

Henry's victory seemed too easy. He had been prepared to throw a few blows, if necessary, and earn the respect he deserved. It now appeared that the only thing needed to end Chauncey's taunts was a single practical joke backed up with some tough talk.

Henry extended his hand toward Chauncey who accepted the gesture with a firm handshake.

"Maybe you can help me put a snake in Charley Stevens' privy," Henry said, smiling.

"He certainly deserves it more than me," Chauncey said, laughing. "That scrote has been hassling you more than I ever did."

With the truce suggesting a new friendship Henry returned to McGary's with Chauncey by his side. As he walked into the dance hall he found his mother sitting at a table next to the back door. Her friends Clara Truesdell and Mary Hudson were sitting next to her. Mrs. Truesdell was holding her hand, and Henry could see that the energy was drained from her eyes. She was gasping for breath, and he knew she needed his help.

"I've been waiting for you," she said, as he arrived at her table. "We need to get home."

Henry helped her stand up and then escorted her out of the dance hall, thanking Mrs. Truesdell and Mrs. Hudson for tending to his mother while he was outside. As he walked her home, he hoped the wheezing would not lead to another night of spitting up blood.

Those hopes evaporated after he arrived at the cabin and spent the night sitting next to her, nursing her through another attack.

The unforgiving nature of the illness caused him to wonder whether she had been handed a death sentence. None of the doctors in Wichita or Denver had been able to help her, and the Silver City climate had seemed her last chance. He did not know where she would go or what she would do next and felt nothing but despair over her chances of survival.

"There's no use looking on the gloomy side of things," she told him that night as she struggled to breathe. "Whatever happens, the laugh's on us."

Henry was astonished that even when his mother was so ill, she could still sense his distress and find a way to keep his spirits up.

November 1873

— 6 —

Henry had not seen Bill Antrim for two months, and his high hopes that he would never see the son-of-a-bitch again were dashed the night he saw Bill coming down a hill west of Silver City.

Henry was on his way to the Truesdells' to play a game of skat with Chauncey. Louis and Sarah had taught him the game, and he couldn't wait to teach it to Chauncey. Now that Bill was coming home, the game would have to wait.

Henry watched Bill plod down the hill, looking at the ground as he walked, his burro strolling beside him. Henry had helped load food, water, mining tools, and a rocker box on that burro's back before Bill left town, and he figured there were probably fewer supplies on the animal's back now than when Bill left. Bill was not the type of man to return from a prospecting trip more profitable than when he began.

Bill was straightening his back and stretching his arms behind his head when he looked up and saw Henry at the bottom of the hill. Henry could see the tobacco glowing from the corner of Bill's mouth as he tipped his ragged slouch hat to acknowledge Henry's presence.

Henry then waited as Bill navigated his way down the rocky

hill. Henry certainly wasn't going to walk up the hill and offer any help to a man who didn't deserve it. The sun had dropped below the horizon, and there was scarcely enough light to guide Bill down. Bill leaned to his right, looking as if he needed to examine the ground in front of him, and, for a moment, it looked like he might lose his footing. Henry hoped the bastard would fall and break a leg.

"Look at all those goddamn lanterns glowing behind you," Bill said, as he approached Henry. "Every time I see this town it looks like more people have moved in. I don't know why anyone would want to live in this grubby place."

Henry turned to take a look at the town behind him and couldn't understand what Bill was talking about. The soft glow of the evening's sunset revealed a valley of piñon and cottonwood trees surrounding a small community that contained an increasing number of eastern-looking structures. Henry figured that if anyone ever wanted to paint Silver City on a canvas or old board, the most striking image would be the trees growing along the marsh. The Mexicans called it La Cienega, and Henry thought it made the town look like a pleasant place to live.

"I certainly like being here," Henry said. "Too bad you're not around enough to appreciate it."

"Is your mama still awake?"

"I'm not sure what she's doing. I was on my way to the Truesdells' to play a new card game.

"I hope she's not awake, I'd just as soon wait till morning to see her."

"Why's that?" Henry asked, not really wanting to know the answer.

"I'm coming home with no money. I've spent time in Pinos

Altos, Central City and Georgetown. I spent a few days near the rancheros of the Mimbres before I headed a hundred miles into Arizona Territory. In all those places I had no luck prospecting and had to take a job with the Longfellow and Metcalf mines in Arizona."

"You didn't make any money working in those mines?"

"I made enough to live on, but not enough to bring home."

Henry figured Bill had wasted whatever he made by drinking whiskey and playing faro.

"Why'd you come back?" Henry asked. "It sounds like the job should have kept you in Arizona."

"I missed my family."

Henry didn't need to see Bill's twisted smile to know the son-of-a-bitch was lying. Bill Antrim didn't give a damn about his family. Henry figured the mine where Bill had been working had probably run dry, and with winter on its way Bill just needed a warm place to sleep. There was no other reason he would return to a family that seemed to weigh him down like a heavy stone strapped to a mud wagon.

"Did you ever hear the story of how I met your mama?" Bill asked.

"Never thought to ask," Henry said, preparing himself to hear about it even if he wasn't interested. As far as Henry was concerned, Bill was just looking for a way to keep the conversation away from his failures at prospecting.

"Hell, you should have been old enough to remember," Bill said. "I met her in the carpentry shop where I worked in Indianapolis. I liked her from the beginning. I had no reason to leave that city but I would have followed your mama anywhere. She told me she wanted to live someplace with fewer people. There were 50,000 living in Indianapolis, and she said if it grew much larger, it would be no better than the Bowery for raising you and Josie. She decided to move to Kansas, and I went with her."

Henry had no interest in what Bill was saying, but figured the lying galoot was primed to talk all the way to the livery stable. Without being rude and walking away, Henry had little choice other than listening

"I liked your mama and didn't want to be without her. We ended up in Wichita. Less than a thousand people in that place. I made good money working as a carpenter and even had enough free time to build my own home — four rooms and glass windows."

Henry remembered the house well. Bill had been courting his mother in Wichita, and Henry had spent many hours at Bill's house when his Mam went to visit.

"If your mama hadn't got sick, I'd probably still be living in Wichita. Poor woman. I tried to help her and bought her some Dover's powder. I was promised it would deliver a good cure for a bad cold, but it sure didn't help her. Nothing anyone did could stop her from coughing and spitting that blood."

As far as Henry was concerned, Bill had not earned the right to talk about his mother's illness.

"If I had known back in Indianapolis that she'd get so sick, I certainly wouldn't have moved to a cowtown like Wichita. I had no interest in playing nursemaid to a sick woman."

Henry said nothing, but was surprised by Bill's honesty.

"It was only when the doctors suggested she leave Wichita and move to a drier climate that I found a reason to keep the courtship going."

"Why are you telling me all this?" Henry asked.

"Just thought I'd lay my cards on the table. You're old enough to know where I stand with your mama. If something ever happened to her, you should know that I always liked being around her. I wouldn't want any misunderstandings about that."

"And I don't want any misunderstandings with you," Henry said. "I think you're a no account piece of dog shit. My Mam's too good for you."

"You need to watch your manners," Bill said. "I know your mama didn't raise you to talk like that."

Henry thought about telling Bill he only showed good manners to those he respected, but decided instead to say nothing and remain quiet for the rest of the walk. He'd give Bill his due some other day.

"I loaded my belongings into your mama's wagon and came to New Mexico because I wanted to help her." Bill sounded determined to finish his story. "I also wanted to give myself a chance to try some prospecting. There's no reason for you to dislike me for that. You're mama had no other way of getting to New Mexico without me, and I'd like to see a little gratitude on your part. Without me your mama would not be living in a town with a suitable climate for her breathing problems. I was the only one willing to help her move out here and the only hope she had of getting better. I married her because I liked her, and she must have liked me or she wouldn't have walked into that church with me."

"The Legal Tender is across the street," Henry said, pointing at the livery stable. The ordeal of listening to Bill telling lies was almost over.

Henry knew that much more needed to be said to make Bill's

story true. From what Henry had seen, the marriage was nothing more than Bill's way of getting control of the money his mother had made from selling the property she owned in Wichita. Bill had talked her into thinking that her boys would have a guardian if her illness ever got the best of her. "Who'll take care of Henry and Josie if something happens to you?" he had said to her on several occasions.

Henry figured Bill's concern for his mother was a load of horseshit. For now, it was better to avoid any arguments and get Bill's burro to the corral.

$$-7-$$

Henry helped Bill stable his burro at the Legal Tender. He then prepared to walk with Bill across the street to the cabin. Bill had other plans.

"I haven't had a drink of *aguardiente* in over a week, and I figure I'm due. Why don't you go on home, son? I'll be there later."

"I'd prefer you not call me son, and you told me you had no money."

"I have just enough for a drink or two and a game of faro. Who knows? I might win enough to justify my absence."

"Nothing can justify you leaving Mam alone to fend for herself."

Bill shook his head and walked away, heading toward the saloons on Main Street.

Henry returned to the cabin, ready to tell his mother that Bill was back in town. When he arrived he found Josie sitting alone next to the fire, sharpening a knife.

"Where's Mam?" Henry asked.

"Gone dancing with the Truesdells." Josie kept his head down, concentrating on his knife, never looking at Henry.

"Did she got to McGary's?"

"That's what she told me."

Henry left the cabin and hurried up Main Street toward McGary's. The last thing his mother needed was to see Bill walk unexpectedly into the dance hall while she was socializing with friends.

Henry arrived at McGary's and found his mother talking to Clara Truesdell. Before he had a chance to get to his mother and tell her that Bill had returned, Bill walked through the back door. When he saw Catherine standing next to Clara he turned to leave, but it was too late. Catherine had spotted him coming through the doorway and had already left Clara to talk with him. Henry hurried across the dance hall to be with his mother. He arrived just in time to hear her speak to Bill for the first time in two months.

"I never thought I'd see someone so familiar try to act like a stranger," she said.

Bill turned to face her. "And I never thought I'd see someone so sick at a place where they're dancing the do-si-do."

"I'm glad you're back. I had begun to think that it was more than just the dead that don't return."

"I apologize for sending no letters. I should have let you know where I'd gone."

"I'll make no fuss about that." Catherine's eyes revealed less forgiveness than her words. "Why didn't you clean up before coming here? You look like an old broom."

"I heard you were here and thought I'd drop by before going home."

Henry hoped his mother could see through the lie.

"You need a bath and some new clothes," she said.

"Unlike you," Bill said. "You're looking good, even though you're a little more hollow-cheeked that usual. How have you been feeling?"

Henry wanted to whack Bill's face with a board.

"Where's Josie?" Bill asked. "Didn't you bring him along?"

"He stayed at the cabin," Catherine said. "He's sitting by the fire, trying to stay warm."

"I hope he's doing well," Bill said, sounding preoccupied with other thoughts.

Henry didn't believe for a moment that Bill cared how Josie was doing and could tell that Bill wanted out of the conversation. Bill turned to look at the door behind him.

"Will you be here much longer?" Bill asked, turning back around to look at Catherine.

"This dance hall is my way of staying distracted from the work I do to put food on the table." Catherine spoke in a soft tone. Henry knew her well enough to know that she didn't want to show her anger in a public place. "I've been too sick to do much work, and I'll admit we've struggled. Henry's been good about helping me get things done."

"We all have our stories," Bill said, scanning the dance floor and avoiding eye contact with his wife. "Too bad that money you made in Wichita is unavailable."

Henry gazed past Bill at a nondescript spot on the wall and imagined thrusting a knife through his stepfather's heart. His mother should never have married the son-of-a-bitch and given him access to the money she had earned at that laundry in Wichita.

"Why don't you finish your dancing," Bill said. "Give me time for a drink or two, and I'll be home later. It's been a long trip."

After a short and uncomfortable silence, Henry took his mother's arm and escorted her out of McGary's.

Bill remained in the dance hall, showing no interest in walking home with the woman he had married only eight months earlier.

— 8 —

Henry and Josie stayed up late with their mother that night waiting for Bill to come home. Henry sat near the fireplace reading a book. His mother sat at the table writing a letter on stationary she had purchased at a store in Kansas.

Josie whittled on a piece of cottonwood and dropped the shavings into the coals at the bottom of the firebox. Josie stared at the firebox and smiled as the shavings decorated the glowing coals with dots of flaming cottonwood flakes.

Catherine looked up from the table and asked Henry, "What are you reading?"

"*Short Stories for Long Nights.*"

"You're not reading *The Death of Arthur*? That's a change."

"Just thought I'd try something different."

"It's about time you changed books," Josie said, as he continued staring at the fire. "I think you've read that Arthur book a hundred times."

Henry clenched his teeth. "Who asked what you think?"

Catherine shook her head and returned to writing her letter, acting as if she didn't have time to listen to her sons quarrel.

Henry closed his book and walked across the room to stand

behind his mother. "When is Bill coming home?" he asked, looking over her shoulder.

"I don't know," Catherine said, as she turned her stationary upside down.

"What are you writing?" Henry asked.

"Don't let your curiosity compromise your manners."

"I apologize. I just wanted to know."

"It's a letter to my mother."

"I thought you told me your mother died in the famine. I thought you were the last of the Bonneys."

"That's right. They're all gone."

"Why, then, are you writing to your mother?"

"So that I can imagine she's still alive," Catherine said, her voice cracking with emotion.

"I would like to see what you've written," Henry said. "I never got to meet your mother and would like to know what she was like."

Though Catherine seemed reluctant, she picked up the paper and read the letter to Henry.

"*I think of you often, my dearest mother. I miss the life I lived with you at Lough Neagh. Silver City is not as beautiful as Ireland, and the charcoal-colored smoke from the smelters has inflamed my illness. My lungs burn every hour of the day. But all is not lost. My sons have found a home. I see no need to move again, although I wish I could bring my boys to Ireland. I wish they could have met you.*"

"I wish I had known her," Henry said.

"Do you know the story of Lough Neagh where I grew up?" Catherine asked.

"I've heard you say you lived there, but I've never heard you tell a story about it."

"In Ireland, when I was a little girl, I was told about a giant named Fionn McCool who scooped up a huge lump of earth and threw it into the Irish Sea. They said that lump of earth formed the Isle of Man. The hole left behind filled with water and became Lough Neagh. Only a myth, of course."

"A lie, you mean."

"No, a *myth*. People need myths to explain what they can't understand."

"And we can't understand everything," Henry said, anticipating what his mother would say next. He had never heard her talk about Fionn McCool, but she had told him often that there would always be some things in this world he would never be able to understand.

"Don't you think it's time you and Josie went to sleep?" she asked.

"We'll stay awake until Bill comes home. No need for you to sit alone. Isn't that right, Josie?" Henry looked at his brother, who didn't respond to the question. "Isn't that right, Josie?" Henry was determined to get a response from his brother and walked toward the fireplace, placing his hand on Josie's shoulder.

"I'm tired," Josie said, removing Henry's hand. "Why don't we do what Mam said and go to sleep?"

"How about we play a new card game that I learned from Louis and Sarah?" Henry asked.

Josie waved Henry away as if he carried a disease.

Henry looked at his mother. "Would *you* like to learn a new game?"

"I guess we could play for a few minutes," Catherine said. "Would you play with us, Josie?"

"I guess so," Josie said, his tone revealing little enthusiasm for the game. Slowly, he pulled himself away from the fireplace and moved to a chair at the table next to his mother.

"The game's called skat," Henry said, shuffling the cards. "Trump suit is determined after the cards are shuffled. The card on the bottom of the deck will tell us what suit we use as trump."

"Jacks should be trump," Josie said.

"The bottom card determines trump!" Henry growled the words at his brother like a dog marking its territory.

"I don't want to play that way."

"You got hold of the little end of the horn, you dumb —"

"Maybe you boys should be in bed by now," Catherine said.

Before Henry could respond, the door of the cabin opened and Bill Antrim walked in. He looked like he might lose his balance and fall over. It was three hours before midnight, and he was already drunk.

"I thought you and the boys would be in bed," Bill said, his eyes surveying everything in the cabin except the three people seated in front of him.

"We were waiting for you," Catherine said.

Bill mumbled something that Henry couldn't understand, although it sounded like he was cursing. He then stepped toward Catherine.

"What's this?" he said, picking up the paper in front of his wife. He then read her letter, his lips forming each word as his eyes moved across the paper. He appeared to have difficulty focusing on the words.

"You're mama's been in her grave too long for you to still be thinking about her," he said, spitting the words out as if he wanted to start an argument. "There's no reason for you to be writing to ghosts and wishing you were back in Ireland."

"I'm happy enough living here. Just wishing you were around more often to see what a good town we've found."

"I brought you here. Isn't that enough?" Bill was beginning to slur his words, sounding as if he could not think of what he would say from one word to the next.

"All I'll say is that the boys and I are building a good life, and we're glad you're home."

Henry had witnessed the situation before. Whiskey unleashed an anger in Bill that could make him violent. But Catherine had learned how to deflect his anger. She knew what to say to keep him calm. He had no response to her tactful reply, and all he could do was shrug and stumble toward the bed. He did not even bother to remove his boots or cover himself with a blanket before he passed out.

Henry looked at his stepfather lying on the bed and wished he had not come home. He also wished his mother could make peace with the violence of the bloody dog as easily as she could with her no-good husband.

— 9 —

Early the next morning Henry started a fire in the Franklin and then stoked the burning logs until the coals were hot enough for baking. His mother stood at the table mixing flour, sugar, and water to prepare the pastries she made every Saturday. Each week she needed more pies and sweetcakes than the last to meet the demand of those who showed up for her weekly sale. As sick as she had been, she worked hard to earn extra money for her family, and getting a fire started was the least Henry could do to help her on this chilly November morning — or any other morning. In helping his mother, he was also doing his part to bring a little variety to the normal diet of beef and biscuits that had dulled Silver City's taste buds.

The nearest railroad was 500 miles away and food supplies were difficult to acquire. Most people in town lived on hardtack made from flour and salt brought in bulk from Mesilla. They also ate plenty of jerky cured by local cattlemen, as well as the cabbage grown all over town that was boiled in water for soup and stew.

"A diet without cabbage can cause your limbs to turn black." Catherine had spoken those words to Henry more times than he could remember.

Catherine's pastries were much better than cabbage. Enough people came to the cabin every Saturday that Henry was well aware he wasn't the only one who enjoyed her baking. She made her sweets with sugar brought from Texas on the back of a mule and sold them as a welcome indulgence for those who showed up to buy them.

She usually made butter to put on top of the sweetcakes while they were still hot. The Truesdells donated cream from their dairy for making the butter, but for some reason they had not yet brought cream to Catherine on this Saturday morning.

"I guess it's too cold to send even Chauncey outside," Henry told his mother, amused at the thought of Chauncey having to walk down the frozen hill outside his house carrying a bucket of cream.

Josie, who had slept much later than Henry, spent the morning whittling, never asking his mother whether he could do anything to help her prepare the pastries. Bill stayed in bed even later than Josie, sleeping off his intoxicated return to the family the night before. When he finally awoke and saw Catherine working in front of the stove he got out of bed and shuffled out of the cabin, providing no information about where he was going or when he would return. Henry was just grateful he wouldn't be around to interfere with the morning baking and hoped he would stay away during the afternoon sale.

"You should set up a shop, Mrs. Antrim!"

Henry recognized the resonant baritone voice bellowing from outside the cabin. It belonged to Harvey Whitehill, a local merchant who showed up every Saturday to buy sweetcakes. Catherine had told Henry that Harvey was one of the most important men in town. He owned a corral, designed buildings, and served as the town's coroner. He was one of the first men to bring his own family to Silver City and was quick to help other families.

Henry opened the door to let Harvey into the cabin and noticed the ease with which he carried his large, muscular frame. He looked as if nothing bothered him, strong enough that no one would ever get the best of him and confident enough that most would never try. Henry respected Harvey. In Henry's eyes, Harvey was a tough but warmhearted man, a man Henry could admire.

"I know I'm early," Harvey said, as he helped Catherine transfer baked goods from the Franklin to the table, "but I've got coroner's work to do this afternoon. There was another man killed at the Orleans Club last night. He died at an ill-suited time for me, considering everything else I've gotta get done."

"In the end, we're all working on God's schedule," Catherine said.

"Did you hear that the jury decided not to charge David

47

Abraham?" Harvey asked.

"No. But I have been concerned about him. Everyone knows he might have got himself in a little trouble."

"The jury decided he was justified in shooting that Negro fella in the chest last week. That fella was on his property, crawling around on the roof of his house. The jury accepted my recommendation and decided not to put him on trial. Mr. Abraham is, after all, an honorable man with a fine family."

"If you made the recommendation, I'm certain the jury did the right thing," Catherine said.

"Well, thank you, Mrs. Antrim. I'm honored to have earned your trust." Harvey doffed his flat-brimmed hat and placed it next to his chest. "Forgive me for changing the subject, Mrs. Antrim. But did you make any pumpkin pies? Pumpkin pie gives me a reason to get out of bed this time of year."

Henry not only respected Harvey, he liked him. He was a man of good manners, and unlike Bill Antrim, he didn't enter a room like a dark cloud.

"No pumpkin today," Catherine said. "Only apple pies again this week."

"One of these days, Mrs. Antrim, I'm going to bring you fresher apples so you can quit making pies that taste like the inside of a chimney." Harvey looked at Henry, smiled, and winked.

"You say my pies taste like a chimney, Catherine said, "but you keep returning every week to my kitchen."

"What else can a clean-living man do for entertainment in this town, except force himself to eat your pastries?"

"It should be entertainment enough watching the dogs run from the sight of that unpleasant mug sitting on your shoulders." It was now Catherine's turn to smile and wink at Henry.

"And they've always said that the prettiest women fall to ugly men," Harvey responded.

"And your wife Hattie is beautiful, wouldn't you say?"

Henry enjoyed listening to the contrast of his mother's Irish brogue and Harvey's Texas drawl. He understood that their back-and-forth teasing came with a spirit of fun, and he was entertained by their good-humored banter. After all, no one with healthy taste buds would ever criticize his mother's pies, and Harvey was too distinguished looking to be described as having an unpleasant mug.

— 10 —

The snow that fell that afternoon should have kept most people in front of their fireplaces. Henry had never felt it turn so cold in Silver City. In any case, he figured his mother's baking would be enough to draw people out of their homes — and he was right.

As usual, more people came to the cabin than Catherine could serve, and she soon ran out of pies and sweetcakes. Henry had thought about making a sign to send people away, but he knew that would deprive his mother an opportunity to visit with those who showed up. She always enjoyed talking with people and getting caught up on all that was happening around town.

One of the last people to show up at the cabin was Clara Truesdell.

"After your cream didn't arrive this morning we decided the weather had kept you home," Catherine told Clara.

Clara Truesdell, a straight-backed and proper woman, had become Catherine's best friend and confidante. On several occasions Henry had overheard the two of them talk about private matters that he was certain were not meant for his ears. Only a few days earlier he had heard Clara tell his mother about her marital problems. "Gerald's a good man," Clara had said, "but I can't bring myself to love him any more. Only the boys are keeping us in the same home."

Henry had also overheard his mother confiding in Clara. "We've lived in some wild places," she had said. "In Wichita we lived on the second floor above my laundry, a good enough place to stay until a saloon they called Keno Corner moved in across the street. After that saloon opened up, the sound of gunfire became as ordinary as the sun rising in the morning, and I feared every day that a stray bullet would strike one of my boys. One afternoon Josie had blood splattered all over him as he watched a constable shoot a man in the back of the head. He's never been the same since that day. I've moved from New York to New Mexico looking for a safe place to raise my boys. I hope Silver City is a place we can stay."

One day, Henry overheard his mother and Clara talk about starting a millinery shop near Chihuahua Hill. His mother knew how to run a business and was willing to help Clara learn how to make a profit. His mother had told Clara that she had money left over from the sale of her Wichita laundry and could think of no better investment than establishing a partnership with a good friend.

On this cold November afternoon, Henry's mother and Clara avoided personal business and spoke only of pastries and cream. Clara explained that sore throats and high fevers had kept her family from bringing the cream that morning. "We've all been sick, and I only gathered enough strength to deliver my apologies. I'll soon need to get back home and return to my bed and hot tea."

"Don't worry yourself," Catherine said. "It sounds like your family has been through the mill, and we had enough apple butter left over from last week to flavor the cakes."

Henry figured that Clara left the Antrim cabin that day satisfied she had not let his mother down. The sweetcakes had all been sold and the money safely tucked away. No customer had lodged a single complaint about the lack of butter.

After Clara left, Catherine rested on her bed while Henry recruited Josie to help him clean and store the cooking utensils. He then convinced Josie and his mother to try playing skat one more time, this time — he hoped — with better results. His mother's proclamation that they would play it Josie's way — making jacks the trump suit — allowed Henry to finish explaining the rules and get the game started without any controversy. When Josie won the game, Henry was ready to play another and get his revenge, but his mother had played enough. She was exhausted from the day's activities and wanted to go to bed.

With Catherine in bed asleep, Josie sat by the fireplace and resumed whittling. Henry, having put away his book of short stories, returned to reading *The Death of Arthur*.

"Would you read me some of that book?" Josie whispered.

"What's this?" Henry asked. "Are you finally interested in something more than whittling?"

"I'd just like to hear a story. That's all."

Henry smiled at Josie's request and began reading in a voice soft enough that it would not disturb his mother.

"Then on a day there came in the court a squire on horseback, leading before him a knight wounded to the death, and told him how

there was a knight in the forest had reared up a pavilion by a well, and hath slain my master, a good knight..."

Henry read for about a quarter of an hour before he and Josie decided to put out the flame in the lantern and go to sleep. Josie fell asleep first. Henry, wrapped snugly in his wool blanket, remained awake, thinking about chivalrous knights and honorable behavior and all that the world had once been.

In the midst of pleasant thoughts about Lancelot and a code that no longer existed, he heard his mother begin to cough. He hastened to her side with clean rags and water to begin the routine of nursing her through the night, a routine that in recent weeks seemed less and less helpful as he watched her illness grow worse.

He watched the light from a candle next to the bed flicker across her face as he held her head in one arm. He left one hand free to hold a piece of cloth for catching blood. As she coughed, he turned her to one side. She was too weak to lift her head.

"Be strong, Mam. Morning will come soon, and tomorrow night we'll be dancing the Highland Fling." He had grown weary of his own words of encouragement. Nothing he said ever seemed to help her. "I've learned a new song, if you want to hear it."

Catherine's sunken eyes stared upward. She was too weak and coughing too hard to respond.

"Sarah Abraham taught it to me. She told me it's sung in the theaters back east. It's called *Silver Threads Among the Gold.*"

He then began singing in his youthful, but expressive, tenor.

"O my darling, mine alone
You have never older grown
Yes, my darling, mine alone
You have never older grown,

But, my darling, you will be
Always young and fair to me
Yes, my darling, you will be
Always young and fair to me."

By the time he finished, his mother had quit coughing and closed her eyes. The bloody dog had gone away, and she had found enough time free of her cough to fall asleep. Henry hoped she would sleep at least until the sun came up. She handled her days so much better after a good night's sleep.

— 11 —

No sooner had Henry returned to his wool blanket on the floor than Bill Antrim walked through the door. From across the room Henry could smell the foul odor of whiskey on Bill's breath.

"I heard that barking bitch all the way from Yankie Street!" Bill said, his voice puncturing the cold air with lubricated rage. "She's keeping the whole goddamn town from sleeping!"

Henry shoved his blanket aside and stood up. "You're the one whose waking people up, and if you're yelling because you think Mam should quit coughing, well then you can just go to hell."

Bill's face tightened in an anger that Henry knew well. "Talk like that might get out of hand without a good thrashing. I wish I had a leather strap to rearrange your manners."

With only the fireplace's smoldering coals to light the cabin, Bill looked around until he spotted a butter churn next to the stove. He then reached to grab its wooden dash. "This'll knock those goddamned buckteeth out of your smart mouth," he said.

Henry could see the fury in Bill's eyes and stepped in front of him. "I'm not afraid of you. You've had too much to drink, and your thoughts have gone crooked."

"My thinking's straight enough to know that someone should teach you a lesson."

"*You're* the one should be taught a lesson. No one wants you around here when you've been drinking. Why don't you go away until you've sobered up?"

"I don't need some pale-skinned runt of the litter telling me what to do." Bill tugged on the churn dash, unable to remove it from the lid. "It's time you learned some manners."

Henry, needing to protect himself before Bill got hold of the dash, grabbed a meat knife from the table, a knife that Bill fortunately had not seen. Before Bill could pull the dash out of the churn, Henry shoved the knife under Bill's jaw.

"I've heard enough from you," Henry said, looking straight into Bill's eyes, his voice strong and firm. "You shouldn't talk to my Mam the way you do. You need to leave this home."

Bill let go of the dash and stood as still as a tombstone at midnight.

"You've been with my Mam a long time. She treats you well, and you don't deserve it."

Henry was discovering something within himself that he had never experienced before. He was ready to kill another person with no regrets.

"I oughta stick you like an old goat," he said. He then stuck the knife far enough into the flesh under Bill's jaw to draw blood. "Mam can't work much any more, and she needs your help, but she sure doesn't need the help of a man who comes home drunk."

Behind him, Henry could hear someone moving around and

assumed that Josie had been awakened by the commotion. He also heard his mother begin to cough and knew she had awakened.

Bill looked over Henry's shoulder at Josie, then at Catherine. Slowly, he stepped back from Henry's knife. Without saying a word he cupped his right hand under his jaw to catch the blood dripping from his neck. As he stared at Henry, the soft glow of burning coals exposed the dark shadows of his face and the contempt he felt for his stepson. Turning his back to Henry, he left the cabin, neglecting to close the door behind him.

As Henry reached to shut the door, he watched Bill walking away from the cabin into the frigid November night. Bill looked cold and alone as he disappeared into the shadows of Main Street, but Henry felt no sympathy for him. Henry did not know when his stepfather would return — nor did he care.

With his mother's coughing drawing him back to the bed, he sat down next to her and began another session of nursing her through an attack of the bloody dog. He held a towel to catch the fruit of her disease and in a whisper began to sing.

> *"Yes, my darling, you will be*
> *Always young and fair to me."*

April – May 1874

Catherine had been at the meeting no more than a quarter of an hour and was already frustrated by Sarah Brown's foolishness. Catherine was sitting with a dozen other women in Clara Truesdell's parlor to talk about reestablishing a school in Silver City. The women called themselves the Ladies Educational Society, and if not for Mrs. Brown's infuriating interruptions, their meeting might have been more pleasant and productive. Mrs. Brown's silliness had made Catherine angry and eager to go home. She certainly had better things to do than listen to Mrs. Brown complain about the town's children.

"We need a school because we need a place to confine our children and keep them out of our way," Mrs. Brown said.

Catherine cringed at the unmerciful tone and the high-pitched squeal spilling out of Mrs. Brown's porcine face.

"What we *need*," Catherine said, leaning forward and looking directly into Mrs. Brown's eyes, "is a place for our children to learn how to read, write, and calculate. We do not need a place to *confine* them."

"All I'm saying is that we should get our children off the streets so they can't cause mischief."

"I wouldn't call playing in the street *mischief*," Catherine said. "They're children. They need a place to play. They can't just sit in their homes all day. You raised two children of your own. You should at least know that much."

Catherine was irritated that Mrs. Brown was keeping the women from accomplishing their task of getting a school started in Silver City. They had been working since late summer and had confronted one obstacle after another. They did not need Mrs. Brown to make their work more difficult.

At first, they had been unable to solicit funds from businessmen who were more willing to invest in new silver mines than the education of children. If not for David Abraham, Dick Hudson, and Harvey Whitehill convincing an association of their friends to donate money, the women would have never raised enough funds to buy books and hire a teacher.

After the women had raised enough funds, they had spent several weeks unable to find an adequate location for the school. William McGary eventually came forward and offered the use of his dance hall during daylight hours, but only on the days that district court was not scheduled to meet in the same building. The women accepted his offer, grateful that he let them use his establishment at no charge, even though its use was limited.

The first public school in Silver City had then opened three months earlier in January with thirty students meeting in a corner of McGary's dance hall. All seemed well during those first days of the school's session. Catherine had sent Henry and Josie to the school every morning, never letting them miss a lesson. As she would have expected, Henry enjoyed being back in school for the first time since they had moved from Wichita. Josie, on the other hand, did nothing but complain, mostly about the teacher.

"He makes me do too many chores," Josie said.

Mr. Webster, the school's teacher, had used a preacher's pulpit as a lectern. At the end of the day he asked Josie to carry the pulpit to the back of the room. He also asked Josie to help other students place their books in wooden crates and clear the floor for the evening's dances. Students stacked the crates in a woodshed behind McGary's after school and carried them back into the building the next day. None of that seemed unreasonable to Catherine, and she grew tired of Josie's complaints.

"Josie's just lazy," Henry told her.

From what Henry said about Mr. Webster, Catherine had decided that he was a pleasant man, although he seemed to possess little ability to present lessons.

"The boys run wild while he's trying to teach," Henry said. "Nobody listens to him."

Catherine was not surprised when Mr. Webster left town and moved to California at the end of the school's first session. "Sounds like he's just not suited for the teaching life," she told Henry.

After Mr. Webster moved away, Silver City's children found themselves again without a school, causing the Educational Society to resume their work of getting one reestablished. After several days of meetings, they had made little progress. They couldn't find a teacher, and Mrs. Brown seemed determined to keep the conversation away from issues that mattered. Catherine had grown weary of the undertaking. She was about to give up and resign herself to continue teaching Henry and Josie at home. With Mrs. Brown's constant interruptions, Catherine was beginning to believe the Educational Society would never get its work done.

"Mr. Owen Scott agrees with me," Mrs. Brown said, her voice rising in volume. "He's been writing in his newspaper that the street Arabs of this town are causing too much trouble."

"Mr. Scott has no children of his own," Catherine shot back, "and he doesn't understand that playing in the streets doesn't cause trouble. I can't believe Mr. Scott's bad manners in calling our children Arabs. Surely you don't agree with that, Mrs. Brown."

"I do," Mrs. Brown said, her nose twitching and jerking upward as she stared at Catherine.

"I haven't heard children called Arabs since I left the Bowery," Catherine said. "The children of this town are nothing like the orphans and ruffians I saw in that place. They survived by begging and stealing, and that is not true of the children in this town."

"Well," Mrs. Brown said, condescendingly, "Mr. Scott is a well-educated man with a refined, eastern sensibility. He wants Silver City to be more than just a mining camp. He wants us to be civilized — an 'oasis in the New Mexico Territory' is the way he described it in his newspaper."

"All of us want that," Catherine said.

"Mr. Scott said our children are untamed and making this town uncivilized."

"For goodness sake," Catherine said, "they're only children. Why is Mr. Scott so concerned with the behavior of our children when the saloons are sheltering the real wickedness in this place?"

"Because the children are running wild and causing mischief! The little devils need to be locked up!"

"We should get back to what we can all agree on," Clara Truesdell said, ending the argument. The tone of Clara's voice indicated she was also frustrated with Mrs. Brown and wanted to make the meeting more productive.

"We all agree that we need to get a school reestablished — whatever the reason," Clara said. "We should also agree that our biggest problem has come from not having a teacher, and I have a proposal. I've heard that Lucretia Pratt needs an income and that she might be willing to teach — if we can find a way to pay her."

Catherine knew Lucretia well. Lucretia's husband had recently abandoned her, and gone to Colorado. Lucretia was a good-natured and educated woman, who often borrowed books from Catherine. She had no children of her own to keep her at home, and Catherine thought she would make a superb teacher.

"Can we all agree that we should ask Lucretia to be our teacher?" Clara asked.

"I have one condition before we talk to her," Mrs. Brown interjected. "I want the school moved out of McGary's dance hall. It's not proper for a school to be attached to a saloon."

Catherine was not surprised that Mrs. Brown would find a way to complicate things. She always did.

"A few days ago," Mrs. Brown continued, "a vagabond pinned a Mexican's hand to the preacher's pulpit with a bowie knife. That didn't happen in the saloon where men were drinking — it happened right there in the dance hall. A place where something like that happens is not a place to put a school."

Catherine couldn't help but question Mrs. Brown's logic. What happened in the dance hall at night shouldn't affect how the building was used during the day. Civic court sessions and church services were held at the dance hall and the place should certainly be able to handle a school. If Mrs. Brown was so determined to get the town's children off the street, a proposal to hold classes at

McGary's should not have been an obstacle.

"Since Mrs. Brown wants us to stay away from McGary's, we'll try and find another location," Clara said, sighing.

"Mr. McGary owns land across from his saloon," Mary Hudson said. "The land has an abandoned adobe building on it, and I can talk Mr. McGary into letting us use it for our school. He should at least let us use it until he finds a way to profit from it."

Except for Clara, Mary was Catherine's closet friend in Silver City. Catherine knew that when Mary set her mind to something, she would not be stopped.

"I know the building you're talking about," Clara said. "It would be perfect if we put a little money into fixing it up. We could try to solicit enough funds from business owners to help us get it ready. I know my husband would be willing to make a contribution."

"Mr. Scott suggested in his newspaper that the town's children prepare theatricals to keep them from causing trouble," Mrs. Brown said. "A theatrical might also be a good way of raising money for the school."

Catherine was astonished that Mrs. Brown had finally offered something worthwhile to the discussion.

"I agree that a theatrical would be a good way to raise money," Catherine said. "It would also be a good way to give our children something fun to do, and we can ask Lucretia if she would be willing to organize a performance. If she decides to be our teacher, a theatrical would be a good way for her to meet the children."

It was the first time Catherine could remember agreeing with anything coming out of Mrs. Brown's pursed lips.

With the meeting finally ending, Catherine was pleased that she might soon be sending Henry and Josie back to school. She wanted her boys to grow up and become something more than miners or ranch hands. She hoped they might someday own a business or a law office. Maybe Henry might even get elected to political office. He was certainly sociable enough. But first, her boys needed to get an education, and they needed more than just the lessons she gave them at home. They needed a good teacher and the opportunity to learn with other students their age. Catherine had no idea whether Lucretia Pratt would make a good teacher, but if Lucretia agreed to teach, Catherine sensed she would work hard and give her boys all they deserved.

— 13 —

Henry didn't like Owen Scott. Mr. Scott's face displayed a look of permanent annoyance, and he never spoke to children unless in anger. When he spoke to adults he glared at them from underneath his brown derby, his close-set eyes magnified by his oval-shaped glasses. He was editor of the town's newspaper and his editorials dwelled too much on Silver City's problems. Whether he was discussing sidewalks or streetlights or the town's idle youth, he attacked community issues with a raging determination to make others see it his way.

Henry had overheard his mother tell Clara that Mr. Scott worked as a government clerk before he came to Silver City. Henry had also heard his mother say that she didn't like Mr. Scott using his editorials to turn public opinion against the town's children.

From what Henry could tell, the success of the editorials was widespread. Adults on every corner referred to him and his friends as Arabs, the term Mr. Scott used in his newspaper. Henry and his friends were increasingly told by adults, usually with raised voices, that they should get out of the street and go home. One day, for no apparent reason, Isaac Cohen prohibited Henry and his friends from playing in front of his dry goods store. Children had always played in front of that store and Isaac had never before made an issue of it. When telling them to leave, he hollered that he didn't need any "goddamned Arabs" interfering with his business.

Even William McGary, who had always supported the town's families, yelled at Henry and his friends as they gathered in front of his house. For a long time the boys had run races on the street where Mr. McGary lived, and he had never once protested. Like Mr. Cohen, he called Henry and his friends Arabs as he shouted at them to go away.

"Why does Mr. Scott not like us?" Henry asked his mother one Saturday as he helped her prepare the oven for baking. "And who are these Arabs everyone keeps talking about?"

"Don't let it trouble you," Catherine said. "I heard that word every day in the Bowery. That's what they called the idle boys getting into trouble — street Arabs. And there were plenty of good reasons to get *those* boys off the streets. They were the worst hooligans you can imagine. You and your friends are not even the same breed as those boys."

"Chauncey and I were walking down Yankie Street yesterday laughing at a joke that Louis made. Mr. Scott stopped us and scolded us. He said we should be in school."

"Did you tell him your teacher left town?"

"He knows that. I don't know why he's using us to grind his axe."

"No need to feel sorry for yourself. It's hard to be heard when you're young." Catherine looked into Henry's eyes. It was obvious to Henry that she wanted to make sure he was listening to her.

"I just want them all to know I'm no troublemaker," Henry said.

"Of course you're not. Some people just assume that young boys will be causing trouble, regardless of the truth." Catherine put her hands on Henry's shoulders. "Don't let them bother you. You were born on the side of the angels, as we all are, and you don't want anything pulling you away from your good nature. You're a fine boy, Billy McCarty, and it's important that you stay that way."

Henry loved when his mother called him Billy. He only wished his stepfather had allowed him to introduce himself to the people of Silver City by that name.

"Do you remember the lawlessness that took control of New York?" Catherine asked. "Do you remember what happened to that Negro man and his family that one summer?"

"No, Mam. I remember very little about New York." Henry was not telling the truth. He remembered every moment of that lynching but had no desire to bring it up and talk about it with his mother.

"It's a good thing you don't remember, and there's no need to describe it to you. I'll just tell you that there's a wickedness in all of us that can unleash itself if we're not careful. I've seen it. None of us start out bad, but there's a dark side to all of us that's prepared to reveal itself if we don't keep it locked up. Do you understand what I'm telling you?"

"Yes, Mam. You've talked about this before."

"I'm just telling you that I want you to stay on the side of the angels. I want you to stand up for yourself and not let others force you to do something you know you shouldn't do. Fight for those who can't fight for themselves —"

"And stay away from the saloons," Henry said, smiling at his mother. He had been listening to her words of advice since he was old enough to remember.

"You're a fine boy," Catherine said, laughing along with her son's good-humored sassiness.

"And you're a fine Mam," Henry said. "The best Mam I ever had."

"And the only one you'll ever have," Catherine said, a gleam in her eyes. "On a new subject," she continued, "the Ladies Educational Society, as well as Mr. Scott, think the theater is the place for you and your friends. We think a theatrical put on by the children would raise money for the new school."

"I know you're part of that ladies group, but I don't think I like much of anything Mr. Scott wants."

"I believe you should look at what's being proposed. I think you would have fun, and I'd love to see you on a stage. Would you consider being part of the performance?"

Henry knew how embarrassed he would feel standing in front of an audience, but he also knew his mother would not take no for an answer.

"It might be worth a few laughs," he admitted.

"People show their character through what makes them laugh and how they make others laugh."

"I'll see if I can get Chauncey and Louis to go along," Henry said, willing to do whatever his mother asked. "Would you feel well enough to come and see the show?"

"For you, I'll muster the strength."

— 14 —

At the beginning of the year, Henry's mother had found relief from her consumptive cough. She had regained the strength she lost during the hard months of November and December. By February she had even added an extra day — Wednesday — to her bake sales.

But by the end of March everything had changed for the worse. Strong winds delivered blowing dust to Silver City, bringing the bloody dog back to the cabin to burn Catherine's lungs. On days the winds didn't blow, the mining smelters placed a canopy of smoke over the town that became her constant enemy. She was unable to do much work around the cabin and was so drained of energy that on some days she couldn't even pull herself out of bed. If not for Henry's help, she could not have placed food on the table for her family, and the upkeep of the cabin would have been abandoned entirely.

In early April, Bill Antrim returned to Silver City after a four-month absence. He told Catherine he was a changed man and said he wanted to do more to help her take care of the boys. Henry kept his thoughts to himself, but figured Bill had simply run out of money and had nowhere else to go.

To Henry's surprise, Bill took a job, working for Richard Knight at the meat market. The income wasn't much, but it was something, and Henry appreciated any help his mother could get. She had certainly grown too weak to make money by baking and selling any more pastries.

Bill had also quit coming home drunk. He may have still been drinking in the saloons — and Henry believed he was — but he wasn't letting his family see him when he had too much redeye whiskey in him.

If not for his mother's illness, Henry would have found Silver City a good place to live. He had several friends to play with, and Louis and Chauncey remained his best friends. He had also been spending time with Louis's sister, Sarah.

"Is this a blossoming romance?" his mother had asked him one day, squeezing his cheek. He didn't answer, but would have said yes had it not been for the awkwardness of admitting how much he liked Sarah.

Josie didn't seem to care about having any friends and spent most of his time alone. He whittled toy soldiers out of pieces of cottonwood root and sometimes joined Henry for a game of marbles. Rarely did he play with any of the other boys in town. Henry was often frustrated with Josie's unsociable behavior, but concluded there was no harm in solitude. It was just his brother's nature, he figured.

The big news for Henry that spring came from the talk around town about opening a new school. Getting the building ready was taking time, but people were finding a way to help the town's children continue their education. Henry looked forward to the school reopening, knowing it would give him more time to spend with Sarah. His mother had told him that a town with a good school had a good future. True enough, he reasoned, although he mostly cared about having an excuse to see Sarah.

Henry spent much time that spring with his friends helping Mrs. Pratt get the new school ready for its first session. She had asked older students, including Henry, to help her tear down one wall of the building. She supervised younger students in whitewashing the other walls. Henry, Louis, and Chauncey repaired holes in the building's flat roof. Businessmen donated tables and chairs, and Henry helped carry them one by one to the schoolhouse.

The Ladies Educational Society had solicited funds to pay for the renovation, as well as Mrs. Pratt's salary. By the end of March, Mrs. Pratt only needed a few books to get the school started, and a children's theatrical had been scheduled to raise money to bring those books to Silver City

Mrs. Pratt organized the performance for early April at Morrill's Opera House. She called the show *Young Silver City* and convinced all the students who had attended Mr. Webster's classes to take part. Henry prepared for the performance with good humor, although he was nervous about getting on stage in front of an audience. If not for his mother telling him he would shine like a bright light when the curtains opened, he may have backed out of the performance. When even Josie agreed to perform, Henry decided he had better lose his nervousness or watch his little brother get the best of him.

That can never happen, he told himself.

— 15 —

Henry arrived at the first rehearsal of *Young Silver City* anxious to see how Mrs. Pratt would use him in the show. He soon learned that she had not planned anything and expected her students to think up skits on their own. It was clear to Henry that she had also made no plans for managing thirty children. She had trouble getting everyone's attention, and when an older boy walked into the rehearsal she showed just how little control she had over young people.

"I'm supposed to paint the stage," the boy bellowed from the back of the opera house. "Owen Scott told me I should join you at the school when all this is over, but I told him I've had enough schooling. I don't need any more of that book nonsense."

Henry recognized the boy as the banjo player whose inept attempt to play *Cream City Waltz* at McGary's dance hall had made everyone laugh. The boy seemed older than Henry, old enough to grow a beard if he wanted. He outweighed Henry by at least thirty pounds.

"Isn't that the fellow they call Sombrero Jack?" Henry whispered to Chauncey.

"His real name is George Schaefer," Chauncey said. "He's seventeen and too old for this school."

"I don't like being called George," the boy snapped, having overheard what Chauncey said. "Just because I left my hat at the door doesn't mean you can't call me Sombrero Jack."

"It's good to see you have the manners not to wear your hat indoors," Mrs. Pratt said. Henry could tell that she was hoping to avoid a confrontation.

"Good manners, hell," George said. "I just don't want any paint dripping on my hat."

"You have no plans to be in our performance?" Mrs. Pratt asked.

"I'm only here because Mr. Scott said he'd pay me to do some painting."

George spoke in a tone that showed great disrespect for Mrs. Pratt.

"You can do your painting while we rehearse," Mrs. Pratt said, her voice twittering nervously. "I've asked all the children to create a skit for the performance. There will be some singing and a few jokes."

"Sounds girlish to me," George said.

"We're just doing what we can to raise money for our school," Mrs. Pratt said.

"Who's that virgin lookee on stage?" George said, pointing at Sarah Abraham who was sitting at the piano.

At moments like this Henry regretted how small he was. A few more pounds, a little more muscle, and he would have already had George lying on the ground with a bloodied nose.

"She's too young for you," Henry snapped, "and she's already got a boyfriend."

"Probably some limp dick," George said, walking toward Henry.

"At least he isn't someone who unloads his yearnings into a sombrero." Henry hadn't missed a beat in his response, but before he could protect himself, George had hit him hard enough to stretch him out in the aisle of the opera house. George then sat on Henry's chest, pounding on his face. Unable to move, Henry absorbed several blows before Chauncey and Louis pulled George away. Blood poured from Henry's nose and lip as he clenched his fists and prepared to rush at George. He went nowhere, finding himself held back by Mrs. Pratt who had grabbed his shirt collar.

"We don't want you around here," Mrs. Pratt said, looking sternly at George and finally finding some authority in her voice. "We're better off without your help."

"What's got you so jo-fired?" George grumbled. "This place is about as much fun as laying the lip to a tramp in the woods."

"You need to leave!" Mrs. Pratt said. Henry could tell her patience was wearing thin.

"There's more fun at the Orleans Club, that's for sure." George strutted toward the front door of the theater. Before walking out he stopped long enough to grab the turquoise and gold sombrero he had left hanging on a hat rack.

"Did he hurt you?" Mrs. Pratt asked Henry.

"I'm fine," Henry said, with blood covering the lower half of his face and staining the top of his linen shirt. "Can we get back to putting a show together?"

"Nothing I would like more," Mrs. Pratt said. "Why don't you clean yourself up while I get everyone started?"

— 16 —

Two weeks after the first rehearsal of *Young Silver City*, Henry stood backstage at Morrill's Opera House getting ready to perform in his first theatrical with thirty other children.

People who came to see the performance paid the usual fifty-cent admission to enter the theater. They were also asked to add ten cents as a donation for the new school.

"It's standing room only," Mrs. Pratt told the children backstage.

The show opened with Sarah performing Stephen Foster tunes on a piano placed in front of the curtain. *Camptown Races* got the crowd singing, and *Beautiful Dreamer* moistened a few eyes.

The curtain then opened to a semicircle of thirty school children dressed in costumes that conformed to no single theme. Most costumes were simply thrown together from old clothes donated by Mr. Cohen. One boy — Henry never learned his name, but figured he was about six years old — was dressed in an oversized band uniform. The audience laughed heartily as the boy struggled to keep his pants from falling down.

Henry served as the Head Man of the show and introduced the performance by bellowing, "Ladies and Gentlemen, for your pleasure tonight!" He then led his schoolmates in singing *Old Mr. Rabbit* to begin an evening of songs and skits.

During the show Louis and Chauncey stood at opposite ends of the semicircle cracking jokes for the audience. Louis received the biggest laugh of the night after carrying a box on stage with liquid dripping from one corner. Chauncey ran toward Louis to catch some of the liquid in a cup. He then took a drink from the cup and said, "What's that? Lemonade?"

"No, it's my Chihuahua's pee," Louis said to a roar of laughter. He then opened the box and a small dog jumped out.

Josie participated in a skit about a mouse frightening a gorilla. Josie's mouse ears, made of pleated paper, triggered a roar of laughter from the audience.

For Henry, the highlight of the evening came at the end of the show when he stood alone in the center of the stage and sang *Silver Threads Among the Gold* with Sarah accompanying him on the piano. The tune had become popular throughout the nation, and the crowd joined Henry and sang along, repeating the last verse as an epigram to the evening's performance.

After the show, Mrs. Pratt calculated that enough money had been raised to get the new school started. She thanked every child for all they had done.

"You were rewarded with laughter and applause," she told them, "but the greatest reward will come from what you learn in school."

Henry's greatest reward came from seeing his mother sitting in the back of the theater. Her illness had kept her bedridden in recent weeks, and she needed Clara and Gerald Truesdell to take her to the theater. They lifted her into their wagon and brought her to the opera house. During the performance, she sat next to Clara, and Henry could hear her delightful laugh rising above the audience.

"It was a night to remember," she told her boys after the show.

Although Bill Antrim was still in town that evening, he didn't come to the theater. Henry figured he was probably at the Orleans Club, little more than a block away. Most likely, he was playing faro and drinking redeye.

— 17 —

Henry had joined Chauncey and Louis to carry the tables from Derbyshire's Furniture Store that Mrs. Pratt needed to get the school started.

"Would you have been as helpful if the circus wasn't coming to town?" Mrs. Pratt asked.

Henry tried to avoid any expression that would let her know what he was really thinking. He didn't mind helping his teacher, but a chance to go to the circus had been a great incentive.

Most of the children who helped Mrs. Pratt that spring did so on a bargain made with their parents. A Mexican circus was coming to town, and parents had said they would let their children attend if they helped prepare the schoolhouse for its next session. Never had the town's children been more willing to do anything associated with school.

"These are the last of Mr. Derbyshire's tables," Henry said to Mrs. Pratt.

The circus performers had arrived that morning, and Henry

was eager to leave. He certainly didn't want to miss the raising of the tent.

"There's nothing else to do," Chauncey added. "Can we go?"

"Of course," Mrs. Pratt said, smiling and waving the boys out the door.

More than a hundred people watched the Mexicans pitch their personal tents at the foot of Chihuahua Hill that morning. The crowd then followed the performers one block west to watch the big tent go up at the southern end of Bullard Street. Behind that big tent the Mexicans placed a cage containing a lion. Next to the lion's cage they assembled two corrals, one to hold an elephant, the other to hold four camels.

The next morning a parade started at Chihuahua Hill and traveled north on Main Street. Henry stood next to his mother and Josie as the parade moved past their cabin. The camels and the elephant carried riders dressed in costumes of all colors. A wagon drawn by four horses pulled the lion's cage. A white-faced clown with bright blue hair joked with Josie as he walked by the cabin. A small band performed an upbeat tune that Henry enjoyed, although he had never heard it before and wondered what it was called. He later learned it was *Himno Nacional Mexicano*, the Mexican national anthem. He loved the tune and whistled it to himself for the rest of the day.

Once the parade moved past the cabin, Henry and Josie followed it toward Market Street. The circus performers then changed direction and headed west one block before moving south on Bullard toward the big tent. Henry and Josie followed the parade for the entire route, joining Chauncey and Louis in gathering up pieces of candy thrown by the clowns who spent most of their time tripping on their oversized shoes. Catherine remained at the cabin, but later told Henry that she had heard him laughing from a block away. She said that the sound of him having a good time had carried above the sound of the band.

Before the parade had begun Catherine told Henry that she felt too weak to attend the circus, and he would have to take Josie on his own. She gave him enough money to pay the entry fees and a little extra for treats.

"Buy some peanuts," she had said. "All I want in return is a good description of what I miss."

"I'll tell you everything," Henry said.

Henry was true to his word. That night, with Josie's help, he told his mother about every moment of the circus.

"The clowns were the best," he said, standing next to his mother who was too tired and ill to get out of bed.

"They had a big box that could shrink the clowns," Josie added. "Clowns as big as Mr. Whitehill walked into one side of the box and then came side out the other as little as Henry."

"We threw peanut shells at the clowns when they came near us," Henry added, "and they squirted water on us."

"They threw a whole bucket of water on people sitting in the front row."

"Louis laughed so hard, lemonade came out his nose."

"Chauncey drank so much lemonade he had to make three trips to the privy."

"Did you try to smoke Chauncey out of that privy?" Catherine asked Henry, making Josie laugh.

"No, but I did put a cupcake on his seat that he sat on when he returned."

"I wish I had seen that," Catherine said, smiling. "Did they have trapeze artists?"

"Oh, yes," Henry said. "We applauded and cheered every time they made a mistake."

"Men were walking on ropes," Josie added. "One of them fell and we laughed when he bounced around in a net."

"Did he get back up?" Catherine asked.

"Yes, and he performed without a mistake the second time."

Henry and Josie ended the evening eating the buttered sweetcakes that Catherine had made especially for them. She felt too tired to join them at the table and remained in bed while they ate.

"I wish the circus came to town every day," Josie said.

"Then it wouldn't be anything special," Catherine told him.

— 18 —

Henry's memories of the circus disappeared that evening into a struggle to keep his mother alive. There seemed nothing he could do as he watched her battle the worst attack of the bloody dog he had seen. He was unprepared for just how hard the illness could strike his mother, and he began to accept the fact that her consumption would probably kill her.

The fear and desperation in her eyes frightened him. He was accustomed to the coughing and bloody discharge, but had never seen her unable to breathe for such extended periods. When she tried to speak he could not understand most of what she was saying. From the few words he did understand, he learned that she had developed an intense pain in her back, a pain that he had never before heard her mention.

Even Josie woke up and asked what he could do. "Is she going to die?" he asked.

"I don't know," Henry said. "I've never seen her like this."

"I wish Bill was here."

"What good would that son-of-a-bitch do?"

"We need someone to help her."

"We need to get Mrs. Truesdell," Henry said. "She's always told me to call on her if it becomes more than I can handle. Mam may die if we don't do something."

"I can go get her," Josie said, slipping moccasins on his feet. He then rushed out of the cabin.

No doubt the Truesdells would be in bed asleep, Henry figured. He was nevertheless certain that Clara Truesdell would come when Josie told her what was happening, and Henry waited no more than half an hour before Clara arrived at the cabin's door with Josie next to her.

"My Mam needs help," Henry told her.

"I'll see what I can do," Clara said, looking first at Henry, then Josie. "But you both should know that there will come a night when nobody will be able to do anything to help her."

Henry nodded, letting her know that he understood what she was saying.

Henry watched Clara place wet towels on his mother's forehead and whisper words of encouragement. Henry, wanting to do something to help, stepped forward and held a dry towel to catch the blood dripping down the side of his mother's mouth.

Nothing seemed to help his mother that night, and Clara did little that he would not have done himself. But with Clara in the cabin, at least he and Josie were not left to face the situation alone. His mother's cries of agony, her inability to breathe, continued until morning.

After what felt like the longest night of Henry's life, the sun rose on a cool morning with his brother asleep on the floor and his mother in bed, too weak to move. Henry sat next to the bed as Clara stood behind him.

"You should prepare for the worst," Clara said. "You're old enough to face the truth about what might happen."

"I never thought it would be this bad."

"It'll probably get worse," Clara said, placing her hand on Henry's shoulder.

Catherine's health declined rapidly after that night. She did not get out of bed for the rest of the month as her friend Clara sat with her during the day, and Henry sat with her during the night.

Bill Antrim had not been at the cabin for over a week. Henry figured that when he realized Catherine's illness was growing worse, he decided to stay away from the cabin. Henry heard later that Bill had left town.

September – November 1874

Henry and his friends ran races up the Market Street hill almost every day during the summer months. The boys in town paired off according to their ages, and the reward for winning was nothing more than the bragging rights that carried into the next race.

Henry never had an opportunity to brag. He had tried hard to win, but his stride was too short to keep up with taller and stronger runners such as his friend Harry, who was Harvey Whitehill's son. As long as Henry lost with a sense of humor, he figured he wouldn't embarrass himself, and he certainly didn't want to embarrass himself because Sarah often watched the races from the top of the hill. Some might have thought she showed up to cheer her brother Louis to victory. Henry knew she was there to cheer for him.

One afternoon in early September, Sarah was watching the races with her friend Emma, Harry's sister, standing next to her. As Henry approached the finish line he could hear Emma pestering Sarah about talking to him.

"Tell him you like him," Emma said.

Emma seemed unaware that Sarah already knew Henry well. Henry was the boy that Sarah liked more than any other, and Henry already knew that.

"Do you enjoying watching me and your brother lose every race to Harry?" Henry asked Sarah. "You've been up here enough to know that the two of us aren't fast enough to catch a cold."

"If you lengthened your step, you might move faster," Sarah said. "You also need to push off with your toes."

Henry laughed at the suggestions. "So, that's why I lose. It's my toes that keep me from winning."

"Your toes and the short legs your mama gave you," Sarah said, laughing with Henry.

Henry looked at Harry and issued a challenge. "Let's run again next week after I practice lengthening my steps. I'm bound to catch you then because I've got Sarah Abraham advising me."

"You couldn't catch my grandmother," Harry said.

"Race me again," Henry said, "and I'll make you look so slow that people will think your shadow could beat you to the end of the street."

Henry had never won a race against Harry and never would. Harry was a muscular boy, possessing too much athletic ability for someone as scrawny as Henry to beat him at anything requiring speed or strength. Henry just hoped his slow stride up the hill would never mean he'd be at a disadvantage in keeping Sarah's attention. As far as he could tell, Sarah didn't seem to care whether he won or lost. She seemed more impressed with the good-natured banter after the race.

"Can I walk you home?" Henry asked Sarah, noticing how the soft blue of her eyes matched the color of her dress.

"Of course," she said. "Do you mind if Louis and Emma walk with us? My father might not like me walking alone with a boy."

Sarah was fourteen, the same age as Henry. Her hair, which

looked like gold to Henry, was tied behind her head, exposing the sharp lines of an angular face and a smile that brightened a room. She was a well-mannered girl from a loving family, and she had a joyful laugh that made her popular with everyone who knew her.

Her father owned a two-story building near Bullard Street that housed a merchandizing store on the first floor. The family's living quarters were on the second floor. The building was made of red brick, and its pitched roof and ornate facade gave it the look of the type of elegant home that Henry imagined he might see in the finer neighborhoods of Boston or New York.

Sarah's mother had died when she was five but her stepmother loved her as her own and provided her with a stable home. Sarah, like Henry, enjoyed school and worked every evening from a book of arithmetic problems. She read every book she could find and played the piano as well as a city girl taking lessons from an expensive German teacher. She taught Henry popular songs from the East, as well as the newest card games. It was Sarah who had lent Henry a copy of *The Death of Arthur,* a book that he had read so many times he almost had it memorized.

For Henry, Sarah was not only good company, she was the prettiest girl he knew, and on this September evening he would get to walk her home.

— 20 —

Henry and Sarah walked toward Bullard Street accompanied by Louis and Emma. Henry knew that Louis was sweet on Emma and had been trying for some time to help him catch Emma's attention. The best thing Louis could do, Henry had advised, was keep his conversation light and fun.

"I'll never forget the look on Mrs. Pratt's face when that roof fell in," Louis said.

He was referring to the recent collapse of the school's flat roof, a disaster caused by a cloudburst that came during a history lesson.

"That mud almost hit Chauncey on the head," Henry said, laughing. "I thought he'd messed his pants."

"I don't think Chauncey thought it was funny," Emma added. "How would you like it if all that mud almost hit you?"

"I sure wouldn't have squealed like a pig," Louis said.

"No need to make fun of Chauncey when he's not here to defend himself," Sarah said.

"You've got to admit it was entertaining," Henry added, "but the screams coming from Chauncey were nothing compared to the noise Mrs. Pratt made. *She's* the one who looked like she messed herself."

Long before the roof fell in, Henry had sensed that Mrs. Pratt did not enjoy teaching in the new school. Every day she showed up at the schoolhouse to confront unruly students, and Henry could tell they were sapping her energy and straining her patience. He felt sorry for her. She had worked so hard to get the school going — painting walls, collecting books, setting up tables. Now, with the collapse of the roof, everything she worked for had been ruined.

Henry would never forget the look of despair on Mrs. Pratt's face. Torrents of water had put a load of mud in her classroom, destroying books and rendering the school unusable. She sent her thirty students home that day with no information about when they should return. Henry heard that she was seen the next day climbing into a stagecoach headed south of town. No one knew whether she would ever return, but Henry doubted it.

"It wasn't the roof that ran her off," Sarah explained. "It was the behavior of her students."

"I showed her nothing but good manners," Henry said.

"I'm not talking about you," Sarah said. "I wouldn't let you walk me home if you were like the other boys."

At that moment, with only a block to go before reaching Sarah's home, Emma's father, Harvey Whitehill, interrupted the conversation. He was standing on the corner of Broadway and Bullard, waving and hollering at Henry.

"I need to talk with you," Harvey said from across the street.

Henry left his friends and crossed the street to hear what Harvey wanted to tell him.

"It's time you got home," Harvey said. "Your mother'll be returning any time now."

"Where'd you hear that?" Henry asked. "She was supposed to be gone at least a week. She only left two days ago."

"I just talked to Dick Hudson. He told me his wife was in a wagon with your mother on the way from Central City. The Truesdells are also with her. She should be no more than three or four miles away by now. She'll probably be home soon after dark."

"Does Josie know she's coming back?" Henry asked.

"I just went by your cabin, and Josie was there. He knows that your mama's on her way. I think you need to get home."

"I will. Thank you, Mr. Whitehill. I'll get home after I finish escorting Sarah."

"There's one more thing," Harvey added. "Mr. Hudson told me your mama's in a bad way. Worse than when she left."

Henry nodded. He understood what Harvey was telling him.

— 21 —

Catherine returned home that evening after having her second trip to the hot springs in the Mimbres Valley cut short. The Rio Mimbres was located a long day's wagon ride south of town, and five months earlier, after her first trip to the hot springs, she had returned feeling refreshed and energetic. Considering what Harvey had told him, Henry did not expect his mother to return from this trip in the same condition as the first.

From the time Henry had come to Silver City, almost a year and a half earlier, he heard people tell his mother about the hot springs north of the Rio Mimbres. Some people had claimed that almost any disease could be cured in those springs. Henry had heard the claims often enough that he began to believe a trip to the Mimbres would burn the bloody dog right out of his mother's lungs.

"The water is so hot," Henry had heard Clara Truesdell tell his mother, "that you can salt a skinned rabbit and drop it in the water to cook it."

Mary Hudson, a woman who Henry thought strutted around like a rooster, was the most vocal advocate of the water's powers. She claimed the springs had cured her husband's gout, and she had no doubts that if Catherine would sit in the steaming water, even for a few moments, her bad cough would go away.

"You should go and sit in that water," Henry had told his mother on several occasions. "It could do no harm."

Henry had seen the Rio Mimbres once, passing it on the day before he and his family first arrived in Silver City. At the time, he was unaware of the hot springs located north of the river. Mostly, he noticed the ranch houses surrounded by cattle grazing on lush grass. On the day he passed the Rio Mimbres, it ran fast with water that he later learned came from the melting snowpack in the southern range. In most cases, he was told, the river ran low and sometimes dry. He also learned that when the water reached the desert it flowed underground. On the day he was in the Mimbres he had not seen where the water disappeared, but he had noticed that the dense grass and towering cottonwoods diminished as he looked down the valley toward the desert.

Had Catherine not been so busy taking care of the cabin and trying to make money by selling pastries, she might have traveled to the hot springs earlier. As it was, she made her first trip in April, more than a year after moving to Silver City. The Hudsons and Truesdells went with her, and when she returned she told Henry how much better she felt. She could not decide whether she was helped more by bathing in the hot water or by breathing air that had not been dirtied by Silver City's smelters. She only knew that she felt better.

She had made plans to return to the Mimbres a month after that first trip in April, but those plans were abandoned when the bloody dog reappeared the next month. Since the day of the circus, her illness had attacked her with an intensity that never calmed down during the entire summer. By September, she had not left the cabin in four months.

"This illness will never go away," she complained to Henry that summer. "It controls my life. I can't talk sense to it."

During the time she was too sick to leave the cabin, Henry became terrified by what the illness had done to her. She sometimes spoke in a way that frightened him.

"Never trust them. They're out to get you," she would warn him.

"I'll be okay," Henry would say, "No one's out to get me."

He eventually learned to tolerate her ramblings as nothing more than feverish delusions.

Nothing he did or said that summer had helped his mother, and he could see that she needed to do something more than lie in bed, sleeping and coughing, waiting for her illness to kill her. More than ever he had wanted her to return to the Mimbres. He understood how weak she was, but even if she needed to be lifted and carried by her friends, he hoped a return to the hot springs would give her some relief from the illness that was destroying her.

"Getting away from the smelters and breathing fresh air can't help but do you good," he had told her. "You should try something — anything. The Hudsons and Truesdells have offered to take you in their wagons. They'll take good care of you. Josie and I will stay home and take care of the cabin. When you return and you're ready to start baking sweetcakes again, we'll have everything ready for you."

Catherine had finally agreed to make a second trip to the hot springs and left Silver City in early September. Henry hoped she would come home feeling better, but those hopes vanished on the evening that Harvey Whitehill told him she was returning after only two days. When Henry heard the news he couldn't help but think the worse. The bloody dog had always seemed determined to win a final victory over his mother, and Henry sensed the time was near.

— 22 —

Henry watched Dick Hudson and Gerald Truesdell carry his mother from the back of the wagon into the cabin and place her on the bed. Henry stared at her emaciated body and was startled by her appearance. He looked at her sunken eyes and remembered a time when her face had sparkled with good humor, a time when she was working in the laundry and greeting customers with warm remarks and a pleasant smile. The cadaverous form in front of him bore no resemblance to the woman in that memory.

Clara pulled a blanket over Catherine and patted the mattress around her to make her comfortable. Henry and Josie stood next to Clara, looking down upon their mother as she slept.

"She's not doing well," Clara said. "The hot springs weren't going to help her this time."

"Is she going to die?" Henry asked.

"We all die someday, and death announces no schedule."

"Maybe she'll get better," Josie said.

"Maybe so," Clara said. "Just knowing that you boys have kept the cabin so clean should make her feel better. I'm sure she'll be proud of how the place looks when she awakens."

"I washed the blankets on her bed," Josie said.

"I can tell," Clara said, patting his shoulder. "Do you boys know where to find your stepfather?"

"We haven't heard from him since May," Henry said.

"You don't know where he is?"

"No idea."

"I realize you boys need help. I'll be here when I can. I'm only a few moments away if you need me."

"Thank you," Henry said. "We appreciate all you've done."

Clara left Henry and Josie alone with their mother that night. Fortunately, she slept until the next morning undisturbed by the bloody dog.

— 23 —

Clara walked every morning to the Antrim cabin to sit at Catherine's side. She worked to keep Catherine comfortable, making sure she had water to drink and soup to eat whenever she awoke. Henry wished Clara could have also stayed with his mother at night, but that would have been asking too much.

In one of the rare moments when his mother was awake and able to speak, Henry watched her hold Clara's hand and talk of her children. "I'm leaving my two boys in a wild country," she said. "Keep them safe."

"There's no need to worry," Clara told her. "Gerald and I will take care of your boys."

"Thank you," Catherine said, barely able to speak.

Catherine received many visits from friends, but usually slept through their time at the cabin. Dick and Mary Hudson came by often, checking on her progress. They never stayed long. Harvey Whitehill, on the other hand, visited every afternoon and always stayed late into the evening.

"You boys have a good mother," Harvey said one night, as he sat with Henry and Josie.

Henry noticed that everything about Harvey was oversized, from his body to his personality. Even the volume of his voice seemed too loud, especially in a small cabin.

"She's a great mother," Henry said, speaking softly, hoping Harvey would take the hint to speak in quieter tones.

"What would you boys do if your mother left you?" Harvey asked, still speaking louder than necessary.

Josie sat in the corner whittling, seeming to ignore the question in spite of the volume of Harvey's voice.

"We'd just do the best we could," Henry said. "I'd like to work and save enough to start a business like Mr. Abraham. He seems to make a good living from his store. His house has a piano and an entire wall stacked with books. He even has enough money to pay a woman to clean and cook."

Henry sensed that Harvey was impressed with his ambition.

"Where do you want to live?" Harvey asked.

"I'd like to stay in Silver City. It's a good town. I like the people here better than Wichita. I like the Hudsons and the Truesdells. You and Mrs. Whitehill have been good to me, and everyone's always been good to my Mam. I'm even trying to like Mr. Scott, although he puts bad things in the newspaper about me and my friends. He just needs something to write about, I figure."

"You've got enough smarts that you should make plans to be an attorney," Harvey said.

"I never thought about that."

"You could help people." Harvey was speaking to Henry in the same tone he might use when talking to his own son. "Too many men have been ruined by money and power, but I don't think that would happen to you. You're only a young man, but I think you're honest enough to use the law the way it should be used. Your mama put good values in you, and I'd like to know that there was at least one honest lawyer out there."

"I'll give it some thought," Henry said. He had never pictured himself as an attorney and was not even sure what an attorney did.

"I've got some advice for you," Harvey added, finally lowering his voice.

"What's that?" Henry asked.

"Beware of alcohol, religious zealots, and whores. You've got a good future ahead of you, but those things will destroy you."

"I'll remember that," Henry said, chuckling at Harvey's advice. "You sound like my Mam."

Harvey walked toward the fireplace and stood next to Josie, towering over the ten-year-old boy like a majestic pine growing next to a shrub oak. "Son, do you know you have a new teacher? She arrived from Texas a few days ago."

Josie continued whittling.

"Are you okay, young man?" Harvey asked.

"I'm fine," Josie said, almost in a whisper.

"Worried about your mama?"

Josie turned away from the piece of wood in his hand to look at the fireplace. Henry couldn't see Josie's eyes, but suspected he was crying.

"Son, I don't know what to tell you," Harvey said. "Just make sure everything you do is a testament to what your mama gave you."

Josie didn't respond.

— 24 —

Henry and Josie spent the entire day getting ready for a visit from the town's new teacher. Clara supervised their work, helping them clean and organize the cabin. Clara had told Henry they should do their best to give Miss Richards a warm welcome.

Mary Richards was an unmarried woman in her mid-twenties. She had moved to Silver City only two weeks earlier, and after hearing that the town needed a teacher, she offered her services to Clara Truesdell and the Ladies Educational Society. The offer was accepted without hesitation.

Miss Richards said she was ready to open the school immediately, and the first day of school was scheduled for Monday, only one week after she offered her services. To get started at such short notice, the Educational Society decided to return the school to McGary's dance hall. The damaged roof of Mrs. Pratt's schoolhouse made that building unusable, while McGary's was ready for students. The Educational Society also decided to give people an opportunity to meet Miss Richards before the school's new session began.

Clara had scheduled a gathering of parents, children, and any other interested citizens on the Saturday before the school reopened. Clara was unwilling to stray too far from Catherine's bedside and had asked if everyone would meet on Main Street in front of the Antrim cabin. It was September, the weather was cooling down, and Clara thought people could gather under the cottonwood trees along the rock wall next to the street.

Henry counted at least fifty people who showed up that evening to meet Miss Richards. As he watched people introduce themselves, he couldn't help but notice that everyone seemed charmed by the new teacher. Silver City might at last have a good school, he thought.

Miss Richards was slender and graceful, dressed in the style of a fashionable woman from the East. She wore a long, yellow dress with a bustle. She was pleasant and well mannered, and her background made her seem like she would be an excellent teacher.

She came to Silver City from Texas, although she had been born and raised in England. She spoke five languages and was related to the poet Alfred Lord Tennyson, as well as John Ruskin, the writer, and Benjamin Disraeli, the prime minister. She even played the piano, having studied the instrument for twenty years.

"This town has never seen so much talent in one person since I moved here," Owen Scott said, smiling and toasting the new teacher. "Very little gives me more hope about this town's future than finding a teacher like Miss Richards."

The activity outside the cabin that evening reminded Henry of the days his mother had sold sweetcakes and people came from all over town to pay a visit. He only wished his mother had felt well enough to spend time visiting with the people who came to meet Miss Richards. Instead, she was lying in her bed unaware of what was happening outside her own home.

Later that evening, after Miss Richards and all the other visitors had left, Catherine remained asleep as Henry sat next to her bed. Josie sat next to him.

"Wouldn't Mam have enjoyed the get-together?" Henry said. "She's told us many times that visits from other people always provide pleasure."

"That's not quite how she puts it," Josie pointed out.

"You're right. She says that some people bring pleasure when they arrive, others when they leave. Either way, they *always* bring pleasure."

Henry and Josie both laughed, breaking the silence of a cabin that had grown quiet after a day of excitement. Their laughter was then interrupted by the beginnings of another attack from the bloody dog. Catherine coughed and spit blood into a towel that Henry held under her right cheek because she was too weak to raise her head. Josie left Henry alone and went to his wool blanket by the fireplace.

After the coughing quieted down for a moment, Henry took his mother's hand and leaned over her gaunt, listless body. "Mrs. Truesdell will be back tomorrow, and maybe you'll feel well enough to eat one of the pastries I saved for you."

Catherine looked into his eyes and said, "I want to see my mother."

"She's not here. She's in Ireland."

"I want to go to Ireland."

"If you go, I want to go with you." Henry clutched his mother's hand as he watched her struggle unsuccessfully to say more.

He did not want to admit that she was near the end, but he knew otherwise.

"I hope you know that Josie and I love you," he said in a whisper.

Without responding, she fell asleep with Henry sitting next to her. Four days later, she died.

— 25 —

The day Catherine passed away began with Henry mixing flour, salt, and water to make biscuits for breakfast. It was a Wednesday, the third day of school, and Henry had been looking forward to another day of Miss Richards' lessons.

When he walked out of the cabin to gather firewood that morning he noticed the sun seemed brighter than usual. The smelter south of town had been shut down for a week and the air was clean. Even Main Street was clean. A hard rain the night before had washed all debris on the street to the foot of Chihuahua Hill.

Clara arrived at the cabin at her normal time and sat with

Catherine as Henry built a fire. Josie, wrapped in his blanket, was still asleep.

"I think you should come over here and be with your mother," Clara said. "Her breathing has grown more shallow."

Henry took a chair from the table and placed it next to the bed. He then sat down and held his mother's hand as she struggled to breathe. Henry could count the long seconds between each breath.

His eyes filled with tears as he looked at his mother. "Let it go, Mam," he said softly. "Josie and I will be fine."

Then came the silence, and Henry knew his mother had died.

Still holding her hand, he said nothing.

Clara put her arm on his shoulder. "I'm so sorry. I know how much she meant to you."

Henry knew he had just lost the one person who would love him more than any other. Leaning over the bed, he gave his mother a kiss on the forehead and said, "I'll miss you, Mam."

"You should wake your brother," Clara told him. "Let him say goodbye to his mother and then take him outside. I'll need to prepare her body for burial."

Henry and Josie sat on the rock wall outside the cabin while Clara dressed their mother's body. Henry tried to read his King Arthur book, and Josie whittled on a piece of wood.

Henry had told only a few people walking by the cabin that his mother had died, but it soon seemed that everyone in town knew. He lost count of how many people came by to pay their respects.

Harvey arrived within an hour and stayed the entire day, organizing and arranging the details of the burial. A pine box that Harvey requested for Catherine's body arrived in the afternoon from Derbyshire's Furniture Store, and Harvey paid the fees.

When Matt Derbyshire delivered the casket he told Harvey that David Abraham had offered the use of his surrey to take Catherine to the graveyard. "We'll need to get her buried by sundown tomorrow," Matt said.

"I've asked Louis Abraham and my son Harry to help Henry and Josie dig a grave," Harvey said. He then looked at Henry and Josie still sitting outside on the rock wall next to the cabin. "Don't you think you boys should get going. Pick up Louis and Harry on the way. It shouldn't take you long to dig that grave."

"We're on our way," Henry said. He had postponed digging the hole, but Harvey was right. If he didn't get started soon, he'd still be in the graveyard after dark.

The next afternoon a brief ceremony was held at the cabin before Catherine's body was taken to the cemetery. Henry stood with Clara and Harvey inside the cabin next to his mother's casket. Josie, not wanting to get too close to the corpse, stood outside with the rest of the mourners — the Truesdells, Whitehills, Hudsons, and many others. The minister stood in the door of the cabin and recited his blessings.

Later, in a graveyard north of town, Harvey said a few words over Catherine's open grave.

"Catherine Antrim was one of the finest women I've known. She had a great laugh and everyone enjoyed watching her dance. Her greatest work is seen in the two boys she brought into this world. A boy is all that God gives us for making a man, and Henry and Josie are good young men." Harvey paused for a moment and looked at Henry and Josie. "I know you boys will miss her, but every time people look at the two of you, they'll know Catherine Antrim was a good mother. That's all she would want people to remember."

After the burial, Henry watched Josie join the other mourners as they left the graveyard. Everyone was on their way to the Truesdells' home for food and an opportunity to share memories of Catherine. Henry remained alone in the graveyard for a few moments, lost in his sorrow. He didn't know until he turned to leave that Harvey had been waiting for him only a few feet away.

"You've got a lot of your mother in you," Harvey said. "You laugh like her. You even look a little like her. I hope you keep yourself straight and make her proud."

"There's no need to worry. I have every intent of making my Mam proud."

Henry then walked with Harvey to the Truesdells' home where he spent the evening listening to people tell stories of the mother he loved.

— 26 —

Henry and Josie continued to live in the cabin after their mother's death. Clara and Harvey dropped by often to check on them. Henry always told them that he and Josie were doing fine.

In one sense, he was telling the truth. His days were not much different from when his mother had been alive. He and Josie would sleep, eat, and go to school — just as they had before she died.

But he wasn't telling whole story when he said that he and Josie were doing fine. He did not tell Clara and Harvey about the pain that churned uncontrollably within him. He could not make it go away, and he only hoped his grief was not as visible to others as the despair he saw in Josie's face.

Josie had grown more quiet than usual, withdrawing into a

melancholy that troubled Henry. At school, Miss Richards asked Josie how he was doing and whether she could do anything to help him. Josie sat in silence and never acknowledged her questions. One day after school, Henry scolded Josie for his bad manners.

"Miss Richards is deserving of answers to her questions," Henry said. "Rude behavior will buy you nothing."

In spite of the reprimand, Josie did not change his ways and retreated even deeper into his own thoughts. Except for the time Josie spent at school, he rarely left the cabin, and Henry could do nothing to get him outside.

Unlike Josie, Henry made every effort to remain friendly and cheerful around other people. It wasn't easy. He wanted his mother back with such desperation that at times it whipped his pain into an anger that alarmed him. Somebody had to be responsible for his mother's death. He did not know who it was, but he wanted to shout at that person. He wanted to hurt that person. People treated him well, showing concern for his welfare and offering their help, but none of that made any difference. He had been engulfed by a storm of unfamiliar rage that would not go away.

He could not erase from his mind's eye the image of his mother entombed in a box six feet under the ground, and he was offended by the idea that people might be enjoying themselves while his mother was lying in her grave. Every night he listened to the laughter and music coming from the saloons on Main Street, but the sounds that were once entertaining now served as a reminder of all he had lost.

"Life moves on," Harvey told him. "There's no bringing the dead back, and we have to make the best of whatever is thrown at us."

Harvey made sense, but his words didn't change anything.

Henry could not quit thinking about his mother. The grief that tormented him would not go away. He felt abandoned and alone.

He was also growing concerned about how he and Josie would make a living. If not for the charitable families who brought food to them now and then, he and Josie might have gone hungry. Realizing he could not always depend on the generosity of others, he searched for a job and found employment working for Sam Eckles at the Star Hotel. The job provided him a small income, but it also meant he was gone from the cabin in the evenings, leaving Josie alone. He had no choice. He needed the money, and Josie would have to make his own way.

Henry hadn't worked long at the Star before he fell into a routine that gave him less time to think about his mother. He attended school during the day, and after school he helped Miss Richards clean up her classroom. He stacked books, swept the floor, and burned trash for Miss Richards, doing anything possible to kill time before beginning his evening of washing dishes and serving food at the Star. Some evenings he stood on a table to sing for the patrons, collecting a few extra pennies to add to his regular wages.

Now and then, he received words of sympathy from the Star's patrons, and he always expressed appreciation for their kind thoughts. But he was beginning to wish that people would quit talking about his mother. He wanted no more reminders, and he certainly wanted no one's pity. He soon learned that nothing worked better at keeping a conversation away from the loss of his mother than a little good-natured teasing of the Star's patrons.

"Good looking hat, Mr. Golding. Did you drop it in the mud this morning?" he said, joking with one patron. Sometimes he would point at the bartender and say, "Someone slapped that man so hard they knocked his clothes out of style."

His mother had told him that his buckteeth molded his mouth into a perpetual smile. While working at the Star Hotel he put that smile to good use. More than once, he overheard the patrons referring to him as the son of that jolly Irish woman. He heard them say he was a well-behaved boy who could make people laugh.

He liked that reputation, and hoped to keep it.

January 1875

— 27 —

Four months after Henry's mother passed away he was still working at the Star Hotel. One cold January night, he had spent the entire evening attending to customers who had grown impatient from waiting too long for food and drinks. The barroom was crowded with men doing their best to stay warm and keep away from the snow falling outside, and Henry could not keep up with their orders.

If he had been given a moment to catch his breath he might have noticed that the filthy, unkempt miner at the end of the bar was Bill Antrim. Bill was leaning over a glass of *aguardiente*, and as Henry walked past him with a serving tray in one hand, Bill spoke the words that startled Henry.

"Inhospitable weather, don't you think?"

The voice was all too familiar to Henry. He stopped and turned toward Bill, looking him straight in the eye. "More than the weather is going to be inhospitable," he said.

As he began to walk away Bill grabbed his arm and turned him around. "How long you been working here?"

"Long enough to recognize the people I don't want to serve."

"Still lacking good manners, I see. Maybe someday your mama

will begin teaching you how to respect your elders. How's she been?"

Henry struggled to pull his arm free of Bill's grasp. "If you'd been around, you'd know how Mam's doing. Where have you been the last eight months?"

"Prospecting. I thought I'd come back and see how everyone's doing."

"We don't need you. You shouldn't have come back." Henry yanked his arm from Bill's grasp.

"Well, I did, and I just wanted a few shots of *aguardiente* before heading home. I wouldn't want to face your mama without having had something to drink."

"Mam died four months ago." Henry spoke the words as if he were describing the weather.

Bill looked down and gazed into his glass for a few seconds before drinking its contents. "I'm sorry to hear that. I wondered if she might be dead by now."

Henry looked over Bill's shoulder at his own reflection in a mirror behind the bar. He was considering what he would do next. If he had been carrying a gun or knife, Bill would already be lying on the floor in a pool of blood.

"Did you move out of the cabin?" Bill asked.

"Still living there."

"Well, I guess it's time to sell it. No more Catherine, no more need to own a —"

Before Bill finished, Henry shoved the edge of his serving tray into Bill's throat. Noticing that Bill was stunned and caught off guard, Henry thrust his shoulder into Bill's chest, knocking him off his stool and onto the floor. Henry then sat on Bill's stomach, pounding his ribs with the serving tray.

It wasn't long before Bill grabbed Henry and pulled him to the floor. Bill then shoved Henry's face into a dirty plank of wood and thrust a knee into his spine. Grabbing Henry's right arm, Bill pulled it toward the back of Henry's head. Henry screamed in pain.

"Let me give you some advice," Bill said. "You should always show respect to those who are older and bigger than you."

Unable to move, Henry was fortunate that Sam Eckles intervened. Sam, the owner of the Star, was the only man in town larger than Harvey Whitehill, and he cast an intimidating presence as he towered over Bill. "No need to prove yourself by pinning a boy to the ground," Sam said.

Bill looked up at Sam. "It's a family concern. I need no advice about dealing with my own boy."

Sam backhanded Bill below his left ear with a lead truncheon he carried to keep order in the barroom. "Get off that boy you son-of-a-bitch and get out of my hotel," Sam said, his tone leaving no room for any discussion from Bill.

Bill, now lying on the floor, put his hand on the side of his head as it filled with blood.

"Get out," Sam hollered, "or next time I'll put a bullet in your head."

Bill pulled himself up, and without saying another word staggered out of the barroom into the snowstorm.

"Get up and get to work," Sam said to Henry. "Too many men need something to drink for me to let you lie around."

Henry's right arm throbbed with pain, and it took him a moment to gather his thoughts before he could get up and return to work. He was angry that he had needed Sam's help and frustrated that he was too little to have taken care of Bill in his own way.

He completed his time at the Star that night knowing he had not yet settled matters with Bill. As he served food to hungry miners, he thought about the confrontation to come and hoped that someday he would be able to get the best of his stepfather.

— 28 —

Henry arrived home after midnight. The cabin was dark when he opened the door. Even so, he sensed that Bill was inside.

"About time you got home," Bill said, speaking in a raspy voice from the darkness of the cramped quarters.

A foot of snow had blanketed the town, and the cabin felt as cold inside as out.

"Doesn't anyone believe in stoking the fire?" Henry asked.

Henry lit a kerosene lamp hanging next to the door and saw Bill sitting on the bed with Catherine's nightgown wrapped around his bloodied head. Josie was lying under his wool blanket on the floor. No one had yet lit a fire in the firebox.

"Nobody's slept in that bed since Mam died." Henry said to Bill.

"You don't expect me to sleep on the floor do you?"

"You certainly don't need to be sleeping on the bed where Mam died."

Bill rubbed the side of his head. "It's hard to sleep anywhere when your head's been cracked open. And that's saying nothing about my ribs. You hurt my ribs, son."

"I'm not your son."

"Then I guess I'll have to take you out of my will."

Bill's scornful laugh irritated Henry. He was in no mood to see the humor in anything Bill Antrim had to say.

"Wake your brother and get a fire started," Bill said. "We need to talk about this family's future."

"What family?" Henry asked. "The family died when Mam died."

"Not much choice but to hear me out. Better wake your brother."

Henry shrugged and walked over to Josie. "Get up," Henry said, shaking his brother's shoulder. "Bill wants to bore us with some us his wisdom."

"I'm already awake," Josie mumbled.

Henry and Josie built a fire while Bill sat at the table, resting his head in his hand, making no effort to help the boys fan the flames. Henry and Josie soon had several pine logs crackling and hissing, creating enough heat to compete with the freezing temperature outside. The boys then sat down next to each other at the table across from their stepfather.

"Sorry you boys lost your mama," Bill said. "I'm sure you miss her."

Neither Henry nor Josie responded.

"I figure I'm going to sell this cabin. I see no reason to hold on to something I'm not going to use."

"What about us?" Henry said. "Where will we live?"

"How old are you?" Bill asked, looking at Henry.

"Just turned fifteen."

"That's old enough to start taking care of yourself. Your mama taught you to be independent, didn't she?"

"Leave Mam out of this," Henry snapped.

"Calm down, and let me finish."

"Josie's only eleven," Henry said. "Do you think he's old enough to take care of himself?"

"I'll talk to someone about taking you boys in. There's plenty of good families in this town."

"I'd just as soon stay in the cabin," Josie said.

"That won't happen. Without your mama living here, I don't see any good reason to hold on to this place. I could use the extra money I'd get from selling it."

"Didn't Mam have money from selling her land in Wichita?" Henry asked.

"We used that money to buy this cabin."

"The money you make selling this cabin should then come to me and Josie. That's only right, and it seems to me that Mam should have had more money than what it took just to buy this place."

"Your mama and I decided to take the money we had left after paying for the cabin and use it to make more money. But none of that's any of your business, is it?"

"It's my business if it's my Mam's money." Henry made no attempt to hide his impatience with Bill's explanation.

"All the money's been given to Mr. Stevens for investment. The money's safe with Mr. Stevens until we need it."

Bill was talking about Isaac Stevens, a man that Henry knew well. Isaac was a prominent businessman in town who served as an ad hoc banker for several of the town's residents. Henry considered Isaac's son, Charley, a friend.

"We need that money to feed ourselves," Henry said, not wanting the last of what his Mam had owned taken away from him and Josie. "We needed it last year when Mam was sick."

"I'm telling you, Henry. What I do with that money is none of your business." Bill seemed to be growing annoyed with Henry. Josie sank lower in his chair.

"It seems to me that Mam's money should belong to —"

"And it seems to me that you should watch your manners." Bill raised his arm as if preparing to strike Henry from across the table. Bill then spoke slowly, clenching his teeth, as if he thought the boys wouldn't understand him without a dramatic delivery of the words. "You boys aren't old enough to know how to handle your mama's money. I'll take care of it until you're old enough to —"

"Seems to me," Henry cut in, "that you're saying me and Josie are old enough to take care of ourselves but not old enough to take care of Mam's money. Isn't that what you're saying?"

"That's what I'm saying. Whatever money this family has is held in my name. You'll get your share when I'm ready, and there's not much you can really do about it."

Henry said no more, figuring there was no reason to argue with the son-of-a-bitch sitting across from him. Bill held all the cards, and Henry knew it. There wasn't much that he and Josie could do — legally.

— 29 —

Within a week Bill had sold the cabin to a man who turned it into a shoe repair shop. Bill had also found foster families for Henry and Josie. Henry moved in with the Truesdells. Josie went to live with Joe Dyer and his family. In return for the care received from their foster families, Henry and Josie agreed to work for food and lodging.

Henry continued serving patrons and washing dishes at the Star

Hotel, which had been renamed the Exchange after Sam Eckles sold it to Gerald Truesdell. The sale guaranteed Henry a job as long as he was living in the Truesdells' home.

Although the new living arrangements meant Henry rarely saw his brother, he heard from others that Josie was earning his keep by sweeping floors and cleaning windows at the Orleans Club for Mr. Dyer. From what Henry heard, Josie was doing whatever Mr. Dyer asked.

After the boys moved in with their new families and the cabin's furnishings were sold, Bill left town. He did not tell Henry where he was going, although Henry later learned that Bill was working east of Silver City in the mines at Georgetown. Whether Bill would ever return to Silver City, Henry didn't know. As far as he was concerned, the world would be better off if Bill Antrim ended up dead at the bottom of a mineshaft.

February – March 1875

—

Henry hoped Josie was staying out of trouble. He never saw his brother, except at school, and they had little time to talk with each other once Miss Richards started her lessons. Henry figured that Josie at least had a roof over his head and the Dyers to care for him. Henry also figured Josie's work at the Orleans Club gave his brother something to do other than carve pieces of wood.

What most concerned Henry was Josie's behavior at school. Josie often failed to attend. When he did show up, Miss Richards had to reprimand him for neglecting to do his lessons. One day after school Henry tried explaining to Josie that he needed to be more serious about learning what Miss Richards was teaching. What Henry said to Josie made no difference. Josie continued missing school most days and ignoring his lessons when he did come. There was little that Henry could do. He was too busy taking care of himself to worry about his brother. Besides, Josie had the Dyers to take care of him.

Henry, unlike his brother, never missed a day of school. He learned much from Miss Richards and enjoyed what she was teaching. School also gave him an opportunity to spend time with Sarah. They sat next to each other in class, and Miss Richards gave them identical lessons, allowing them to work together during the times Miss Richards was helping younger children. Henry was good at working with numbers. Sarah was good at reading and writing.

They ate lunch together, sitting next to the Keystone Hotel behind McGary's and sharing conversation about the books they had been assigned. Miss Richards had asked Henry to read *Ragged Dick*, and he was enjoying its setting, if not the story.

"The book's good enough," he told Sarah, "but it needs more adventure."

"What's it about?" Sarah asked.

"It's about a poor street fellow named Ragged Dick. He's got good values, and good things come his way. He saves the child of a wealthy industrialist and reaps the benefits."

"Even vagabonds can improve themselves," Sarah said, showing Henry that she had caught on to the point of the book.

"Only if they keep themselves on a virtuous path," Henry added. "It's a good message, as far as I can tell."

What Henry most enjoyed about the book never came up in the conversation. He liked that it was set in New York and made him think about what his life might have been like had his mother not moved west. He had been too young to remember much about New York and wished he could talk to his mother about the book. He wanted to know whether she would have thought the Ragged Dick story was accurate in how it described the city.

Miss Richards had asked Sarah to read *Frankenstein*, a book that was causing Sarah problems at home.

"My father found out I'm reading it and said he wanted to talk with Miss Richards," Sarah told Henry.

"Why's that?" Henry asked.

"He thinks the book is inappropriate for school, but I don't think he's even read it."

"Seems to me like it tells a good story. I wish Miss Richards had asked me to read it."

"My father's just watching out for me, I guess."

"You should be glad you have someone who cares about you."

"I am," Sarah said. "I'm sure you miss your mother. I know I miss mine."

Henry had nothing to add. He missed his mother more than he knew how to say and thought it best not to talk about her because he might get emotional.

"My stepmother told me you're the only boy in town she doesn't mind me talking to," Sarah said.

"I guess it's a good thing I'm not a hideous creature like the one in your book."

"Oh, not at all. She told me you seem to be a well-mannered young man."

"If only she knew," Henry said, laughing.

"Yes, if only she knew," Sarah said, taking hold of Henry's hand.

He showed up early every day for school to read and work on his lessons. He then stayed late every day to help Miss Richards with chores after school. In the evenings, he went to work at the Exchange, losing himself in the cheerful banter of the hotel's patrons. He had little time to spend with his friends, but from what he had heard about the shenanigans some of them were getting into, he was glad he had other things to do.

— 31 —

Henry was not part of the problem described in Owen Scott's newspaper stories. Even so, the stories bothered him. Mr. Scott continued attacking street Arabs in his paper, sparking outrage about the lawlessness that came from idle boys roaming the streets. Henry felt that too many editorials on the subject had everyone thinking the biggest problem in Silver City was its children. He agreed with what his mother had said on the issue — the drunkenness and violence in town was more serious than boys spending their time running races and playing games in the streets.

Unlike many other boys in town, Henry had no time to fritter away by running around with friends, but he did spend much time with one friend — Chauncey Truesdell. Not only did Henry live with Chauncey's family, but Chauncey's father now owned the Exchange and was paying both Henry and Chauncey to work there after school. They worked all day on the weekends. After spending so much time together, Chauncey had become more of a brother to Henry than Josie.

Chauncey made a good partner for Henry at the Exchange. Together, they served food and drinks. They washed and dried the dishes that had been dirtied by hungry miners and cattlemen. They also kept up on the town's gossip. The more the men in the barroom drank, the more they talked. Rumors ran rampant, and no newspaper could have kept up with the stories that Henry and Chauncey heard every night while they were working.

"Did you hear about what Louis and Charley did last week?" Chauncey asked one evening, as he and Henry stood in the kitchen scrubbing food off grimy plates.

"What's that?" Henry asked.

"Sombrero Jack's been in town. Louis and Charley have been spending time with him."

"That's not good," Henry said. "Jack's a fellow who will get those boys in trouble. I hate to see Louis go down that road. Sarah wouldn't like seeing her own brother go bad."

"They were outside Charlie Sun's laundry when Jack started doing his imitation of the way Chinamen talk."

"So. What's new?" Henry asked. "Everyone has a version of ching-chonging like a Chinaman."

"But there's more to it. While they were standing around laughing, some coolie came out the back door with trash to burn. Jack threw a rock and hit that slanty-eyed fella square above the right ear."

"Why'd he do a thing like that?"

"Meanness, I guess. I don't really know. Louis told me the Chinaman dropped like a bag of onions and then flopped around like a chicken with its head cut off."

"Did he die?"

"I don't know. Louis told me they ran off before finding out what happened. It's been a week and there's been no mention of anything in Mr. Scott's newspaper."

"Mr. Scott wouldn't write about harm done to a Chinaman. He rarely even writes about the Mexicans on the Hill." Henry put the last clean dish on the shelf in front of him.

"Louis told me that Sombrero Jack thought watching the Chinaman drop was funnier than watching a cat getting skinned. Jack seemed not to care whether he had hurt someone."

"I hope Louis didn't think it was funny."

"Louis told me he felt bad for the Chinaman."

"It's good Louis thinks that. I see no humor in Sombrero Jack's meanness."

"Can't imagine any of those Abrahams being mean."

"Certainly not Sarah," Henry said.

"I don't mean to change the subject," Chauncey said, "but have you seen Charley Stevens lately?"

"Only in school. Not enough to talk with him."

"Charley told me he had a proposition for you. He wanted me to tell you that he needed to see you."

"What's the proposition?"

"I don't know."

"If you see him again, tell him to come by the meat market after midnight when I'm done with work."

"I'll do that," Chauncey said, handing Henry the last tray of dirty shot glasses.

After work that night Henry headed for Mr. Knight's Meat Market where he had been sleeping for two weeks. A rash of nighttime thefts had victimized the town and many business owners were sleeping in their stores with guns by their sides. Richard Knight, who had left town to visit his mother in Texas, had hired a man to run his meat market during the day. But he still needed someone to watch the place at night. He had hired Henry upon Gerald Truesdell's recommendation.

"Not much to steal at night," Richard had told Gerald, "but I don't like the thought of someone trying to break in. Trespassing doesn't set well with me."

"Henry McCarty's the best you'll find," Gerald had said, putting his arm on Henry's shoulder. "He's the only one who ever worked for me that never tried to steal anything. If you can't trust this boy, you can't trust anyone."

<h2 style="text-align:center">— 32 —</h2>

Henry slept on an old cot at the meat market that was about as comfortable as a jagged rock in the desert. Even so, he usually had no trouble falling to sleep after a long evening at the Exchange. He hadn't been in bed long on a chilly night in February when Charley Stevens and Harry Whitehill came to visit.

"Open the door!" Charley said. Charley was rapping on a windowpane as Harry stood next to him in the alley behind the meat market. "Open the goddamned door, McCarty. It's cold out here."

Henry was half asleep and the knocking sounded like a woodpecker tapping at his brain. Finally, realizing someone was trying to get his attention, he got off his cot and opened the door. Charley and Harry stood outside with their hands in their pockets, shivering.

"What are you two doing? It's freezing out there," Henry said, motioning his friends inside.

"Is this all Mr. Knight can give you, a raggedy old cot in a room not much bigger than my papa's buckboard?" Charley said.

"I'm doing the man a favor, and he's paying me for my time," Henry said. "Besides, I've got a fire to keep me warm, which is better than you two can say. What are you doing out so late?"

"We didn't want anyone to see us," Harry said.

"What do you want?" Henry asked, trying not to show his annoyance at Charley and Harry for waking him up in the middle of the night.

"Do you know Old Man Derbyshire?" Charley asked.

"Yes, he built the pine box they laid my Mam in."

"He keeps the money from his furniture store in a cloth pouch he hides under the counter," Harry said.

"We figured we'd swipe that pouch tonight, if you wanted to join us," Charley added.

"What makes you think I'd want to be part of something like that?" Henry asked.

"You're a good sort," Charley said. "We figured a little money might give you a way out of having to work in the evenings. We hear Josie's been making a good living running numbers at the Orleans Club and has become quite the gambler. You could spend more time with him and let him teach you what he's learned. You'd have more time for having fun."

"Leave me out of it," Henry hoped the tone of his voice would end the discussion.

"There's an entrance into Derbyshire's store by dropping down the chimney," Harry said. "We're both too big, but I bet you weigh no more than a hundred pounds and could climb down that chimney with no trouble."

"So that's why you're really here," Henry said. "You're needing a little fellow to help you do your deed."

"Just wondered if you wanted to join us," Charley said. "We'd split the money three ways."

"Leave me out of it."

"Lacking the nerve?" Charley asked.

"Never did have the nerve to steal, and I certainly have no need to take Mr. Derbyshire's money — or anybody else's."

118

"No one will ever know," Charley said. "They won't even be able to figure out how we got into the building."

"I got no use for stealing. Mr. Derbyshire was good to me when my Mam died, and I have this job because Mr. Truesdell said I could be trusted. I have no need to betray people who've been good to me."

"That money would give you time for a little more fun. You wouldn't have to work all the time," Harry said.

"I don't want that type of fun," Henry said. He was growing tired of telling them he wasn't interested in their proposition. "I told Mr. Truesdell I'd help paint the outside of the Exchange tomorrow, and I need my sleep. It's best you two left."

Henry motioned the boys toward the door.

"We know you'll keep this to yourself," Charley said, as he stepped outside.

"Just leave me out of it," Henry said, shutting the door on his friends.

Henry returned to his cot wondering why Charley and Harry, two boys from good families — families with money — would want to steal from Matt Derbyshire. Charley's father, Isaac Stevens, owned mining claims in the area and had invested in businesses all over town. Harry's father was Harvey Whitehill, a man who owned enough property that he had no problem creating a comfortable life for his family. Neither boy had a reason to steal, and Henry couldn't understand their motivation.

Just looking for a little excitement, he figured. If so, it wasn't the type of excitement he wanted.

— 33 —

Someone broke into Matt Derbyshire's furniture store the night after Charley and Harry visited Henry. The thieves stole five dollars and two bottles of whiskey that Mr. Derbyshire kept under the counter. Henry assumed Charley and Harry were responsible.

Had it not been the fourth case of nighttime burglary in less than a week, the crime might not have caused much of an uproar. As it was, most people in town were outraged by the thievery. Businessmen were up in arms, and Henry overheard the patrons at the Exchange making every suggestion imaginable about what should be done to stop the stealing. In one way or another, the suggestions revolved around the harsh punishments that should be meted out to those who were guilty.

Henry seemed to be the only one in town who believed Charley and Harry had stolen from Matt Derbyshire, and he kept his beliefs to himself. The other crimes were a mystery to Henry. For all he knew, Charley and Harry might have been responsible, but he hadn't heard and didn't care to find out.

If Charley and Harry were guilty of committing those crimes, Henry hoped they would keep their guilt to themselves and not share any more information with him about what they were doing. They were his friends, and he'd never get them in trouble. Not knowing whether they broke into other businesses would keep him from having to tell more lies than necessary to protect them. He especially didn't want to get Harry in trouble. He liked Harry. He had run races against him, and Harry's father had been good to him when his mother died.

The town's merchants were angry about the crimes and held a

meeting in the dining room at the Exchange two days after the theft at Derbyshire's. The discussion included elected officials and other interested citizens. Everyone was determined to stop the stealing.

Henry, who was helping get things organized for serving food and drinks at the Exchange, stood in the kitchen and listened to the proceedings, unseen to those at the meeting. Chauncey stood next to him.

Sheriff McIntosh began by telling everyone that he and his deputy had been taking turns walking the streets at night. "As far as I can tell, the businesses that were set upon had their doors locked during the nights of the stealing. We never saw anyone trying to get inside any store."

Henry knew the sheriff well. He came often to the Exchange and always treated Henry with respect. He was a muscular man with enough heft in his upper body that he could probably knock a mule off its feet. He wore a dark three-piece sack suit that made him look like a banker rather than a sheriff.

"I bet it's some hooligan boys," one man yelled out.

Henry recognized the voice as Owen Scott's and pictured Owen pushing his eyeglasses up his pointed nose and squinting as he pontificated about the town's problems.

Henry rolled his eyes and whispered to Chauncey, "I knew that son-of-a-bitch Mr. Scott wouldn't be able to keep his snout out of the conversation."

"I've been writing editorials about how we shouldn't let boys stand around with nothing to do," Owen said. "We need to get these Arabs off the streets."

"I could hire another deputy to keep an eye on things," the sheriff said, "but I'll need businesses to donate money for the extra time my deputies spend walking the streets at night."

"I'd support that," Owen said. "Put me down for a contribution. But I want some return for my investment. I want you to lock up those who've already committed crimes. Do you have any idea who you should be arresting?"

"No idea," the sheriff said. "There's so many miners and cowboys in and out of this town that it's hard to know who's coming and who's going, much less who's stealing anything."

"Has anyone thought about checking on the Antrim boys?" Owen asked. "Mrs. Antrim's in her grave and Bill Antrim's been out of town. That's a perfect situation for those two boys to get into trouble."

Henry looked at Chauncey with raised eyebrows. "How'd Josie and I get pulled into this?" he asked.

"I've got no reason to check on those boys," the sheriff said.

"We've all seen the mischief in the eyes of the older boy," Owen added. "I've never put his name in my paper, but that boy is the lead character in my village Arab stories."

Henry wondered how he could be the lead character in those stories when all he ever did was go to school and work at the Exchange.

"That's ridiculous," Gerald Truesdell called out. "The boy you're talking about lives with me and Clara. He works here at the Exchange. He goes to school and has no time to get himself into trouble. He's as honest a boy as I know. I trust him as much as my own son."

"Maybe you've just been hiding your ears from the rumors," Owen said.

"What rumors?" Gerald asked.

"Isaac, tell Gerald what you've told me," Owen said.

Henry assumed Owen was referring to Isaac Stevens — Charley's father and Harry's uncle — and when he heard the voice answering the question he knew was right.

"I've been told that Henry Antrim's been making trouble since his mama died. I heard he's the one who hit that Chinaman with a rock. It's no big thing to hurt a coolie, but it's still more mischief than we want in this town. I also heard that Henry's the one been stealing from the businesses late at night."

Henry was stunned by what Isaac was saying. What had he ever done to be the target of such accusations?

"We need to tell them you had nothing to do with hurting that Chinaman," Chauncey said to Henry.

Henry put his finger to his lips to silence Chauncey. Speaking in a whisper, Henry said, "If you speak for me you'll have to tell them that Louis has been getting into trouble with Sombrero Jack, and you don't want to get Louis in trouble. Besides, no one can ever prove I did anything wrong."

Henry then heard Gerald Truesdell speak again.

"I don't know who's been talking to you," Gerald said, "but I'll vouch for that boy. Everything I see in him tells me he's as trustworthy as he can be."

"From what I've heard," Isaac said, "that boy has not been staying with you recently. I respect your judgment, Gerald, but it may be that you don't know everything he's been doing."

"Before we start laying the guilt on anyone, I need some verification," Sheriff McIntosh said. "Isaac, who's been telling you that Henry Antrim's a thief?"

"All you need to know is that I trust the people who been

talking to me."

Isaac was just keeping his own son Charley out of the conversation, Henry figured.

"I'll need more information than that," the sheriff said. "I can't lock up a boy on rumors. Why don't I just hire another deputy to walk the streets, and we'll see what happens?"

"I guess that'll have to do," Owen said. "I'll write an editorial telling people how to keep our town safe. Maybe we can end the thievery before it gets worse. Maybe we can bring a little civilization to this place."

"I want your deputies to keep their eyes on that Antrim boy," Isaac said to the sheriff.

"I believe his name's McCarty," the sheriff said, "but, yes, I'll keep my eye on him."

Henry was pleased that the meeting at least ended with everyone reminded that his name was McCarty and not Antrim.

— 34 —

False accusations about Henry ran rampant through town.

"People say you're a thief," said one scruffy miner at the Exchange. "They say you killed a Chinaman. They're saying Henry Antrim should be locked up."

"I've committed no crimes," Henry said, "and Antrim's my stepfather's name. My name is McCarty, and it wouldn't do you any harm to respect someone's name."

"Respect? For a thief?"

"Leave the boy alone," Gerald Truesdell said, walking up to the miner. "He's as innocent as a newly laid egg, and I'll vouch for him.

He's stole nothing and killed no one."

With so much inaccurate information spreading through town, Henry couldn't help but think of his mother's words. "Whatever happens, the laugh's on us," she used to say. Henry figured he might as well smile at what people were saying and then get on with his business. There wasn't much else he could do. Most people were going to believe what they wanted, no matter what he told them.

At least Gerald and Clara were defending him, telling others he was a boy they could trust. Harvey Whitehill also gave him the support he needed.

"From what I heard, this town's putting you through a ringer," Harvey said one evening at the Exchange. Harvey came often to the Exchange for dinner and usually ate alone, sipping on a bowl of soup as he sat at a table next to a window. He seemed to take pleasure in looking across the street at Legal Tender Corral and the outer edge of Silver City.

"How have you been dealing with those accusations against you?" he asked Henry.

"I'm fine. I did nothing wrong, and Mam told me there was no use looking on the gloomy side of things."

"Isaac tells me you're a thief, and he's my own brother-in-law. But if you tell me the accusations are wrong, I'll believe you."

"I'm telling you, Mr. Whitehill, I had nothing to do with stealing anything. I swear that's the truth."

"That's good enough for me. Do you know who we should be blaming?"

Henry didn't answer, figuring Harvey was better off not knowing that his own son and nephew were responsible.

"I guess it wouldn't be right to turn in a friend, would it?"

Harvey said.

"I'll just say I had nothing to do with it."

"I know you're working right now," Harvey said, "but I'd like to talk with you. Would Gerald mind if you took a break and joined me for a bowl of soup?"

"There's no harm in taking a break. Besides, there's not many people to serve tonight."

"Well, then, get yourself some coffee and a bowl of that beef and cabbage soup from the kitchen."

Henry left for the kitchen and soon returned with soup and coffee. As he joined Harvey at the table to eat his dinner, he remembered how well Harvey had treated him when his mother died. No one, except Clara Truesdell, had helped him more than Harvey during the final days of his mother's life.

"Look out that window," Harvey said, pointing at Hudson Street. "Just four or five years ago we had Apache attacking us almost every day. They would watch the street from that hill over there, and if a man came down the road alone, the Indians would make their way to those bushes by the corral and ambush him."

"I'm glad those days are over," Henry said.

"Across the street and next to that corral is where they had a meeting to name the town. They said they wanted a town with no quarreling or jumping claims. They wanted this place to last a long time. I wasn't there, but they told me all about it after I arrived a few weeks after the meeting. I helped create the layout of the town. We tried to make it like an eastern city. We also made a big mistake."

"What's that?" Henry asked.

"We thought those springs running north and south along the base of the hill would make a good place for our Main Street and the business district. What we didn't think about was how all the water running into the arroyos and bringing water into that marsh would wash the street away. Someday a big flood will take away everything that people have been trying to build since I got here."

"Is this what you wanted to talk to me about?" Henry asked.

Harvey looked away from the window and straight into Henry's eyes. The tone of his voice changed to that of a concerned father.

"You're one of the brightest young men I've met," Harvey said. "You've got your mama's spirit and her sense of fun. You might be the smallest rat in the litter, but there's something about you that makes people notice you."

"What's all this about?" Henry asked.

"I'm just trying to tell you that you're one of those types that seems to have a light shining on them. Don't ask me why, but some people are just more noticeable than others. You're one of those noticeable types. With some boys, only their families know their names. But everyone knows you. When something happens, people will naturally think about you first."

"Is that why people been treating me like I'm a thief?"

"That's about it. Those boys that people been calling Arabs? Those boys flock around you like you're the goddamned queen bee. Goes back to when your mama treated them to cookies and sweetcakes after school. Everyone sees that you're the Head Man. They saw it when you were on stage. They saw it when you were running races, even though you were losing. When Owen Scott writes stories about boys being troublemakers, people are going to think about you because you seem to be the chief with all those other boys."

"But why would they think I'm a troublemaker?"

"You're an orphan. People are going to assume you're headed for trouble. It's in the nature of things. Owen has put the idea in people's minds that we got a problem with undisciplined boys. You're the one they're going to think about first. Whether you done anything wrong makes no difference."

"All I can say is I never stole anything."

"I believe you. I also believe you know who's been doing the stealing. You could tell me now and save yourself a lot of grief."

Henry said nothing.

"I'm guessing that you not only know who the thieves are, but they're probably friends of yours. I'm betting you just don't want to sell your friends down the river."

"Mam told me to never break faith with a secret."

"I can understand that. Some might even say there's honor behind your silence."

"Can you help me?" Henry looked down, staring at his bowl of soup. "Can you help me end the accusations?"

"All you need to do is tell the sheriff who the real thieves are."

Harvey reached across the table to lift Henry's chin and look into his eyes.

"I can't do that," Henry said. "I'm not trying to be noble. I know I'm supposed to take care of myself, but I couldn't live with myself doing something like that."

"Not much you can do, then. Just keep out of trouble and hope that people eventually see that you're on the right side of things."

"Will that happen?"

"I have no doubt. It may take time, but I'll vouch for you. We'll just have to wait and see which way the wind blows this thing."

— 35 —

The mystery of the nighttime burglaries appeared solved the day Charley Stevens walked into David Abraham's mercantile store. Louis Abraham had heard the story from his father and passed it on to Henry before school.

"Charley walked into the store to buy a linen handkerchief," Louis told Henry. "He said he wanted the expensive one hemmed with ornate gold stitches. He told my father he wanted it for a girl."

"He only wishes he had a girl," Henry said.

"Charley's been pining for Emma," Louis said. "But I'll lay claim to Emma before Charley ever will."

"Charley knows about you and Emma, but I guess he has no scruples, and I'm not sure how we ever figured on him being a friend."

"You especially won't think he's a friend after I tell you what he did. When my father asked him what he'd done to get enough money to buy a handkerchief, he said it was his own money. He said he could use it as he pleased. He said he earned it doing work. My father asked him what work he'd been doing to make so much money. Father said it was Charley's hesitation in answering the question that triggered suspicions."

Henry figured that Charley was just hesitating while figuring out how to frame his lies.

"Charley said he'd been cleaning the fireplace at his house," Louis said. "My father asked him why he'd get paid to do an everyday chore in his own home."

Henry guessed the question must have made Charley feel as transparent as a windowpane. Charley had stolen the money, plain and simple, and Henry knew that.

"Charley told my father that *you* stole the money," Louis said. "He said you stole it from the furniture store."

"I hope *you* don't believe that."

"Of course I don't believe that. I know you wouldn't steal anything. I think Charley just blurted out your name because people were already suspicious of you."

"What else did Charley say?"

"He said that you had given him the money to keep safe until the accusations against you went away. He said you would let him keep half. All he had to do was keep it in a safe place."

"Did your father believe him?" Henry asked.

"I'm afraid so. My father grabbed his arm and took him down the street to talk to his father. Charley told Mr. Stevens the same tale, and then Mr. Stevens and my father marched Charley down to Mr. Derbyshire's store. Charley then told Mr. Derbyshire about you stealing the money."

"They should have come and talked to me about it," Henry said. "I would have told them I'd done nothing wrong. I bet Charley wouldn't have been able to tell a lie with me looking at him."

"I'd bet that's true," Louis said. "Charley ended up returning the money to Mr. Derbyshire and telling everything he knew about the burglary."

"Did he talk about anybody other than me?" Henry asked.

"Just you," Louis said. "You're the only thief, according to Charley. He said you had a plan to steal from merchants all over town. He said you wanted him to help and that you had it all planned out. Charley was supposed to keep watch while you crawled down chimneys. No one would see the two of you late at night. Charley said that you two would split the money."

As Louis was talking, Henry wondered if liars like Charley ever ended up believing their own fibs.

"Charley said he never went along. He said he got cold feet and only held on to Mr. Derbyshire's money because you had him hypnotized."

Henry laughed out loud. "Surely no one believes something so silly."

"They're certainly believing you stole the money. My father told me he reported everything to the sheriff, and the sheriff wants to talk with you today after school."

"I hope you know that everything Charley said is a lie."

"I know he's lying. But you need to prepare to defend yourself from what others are saying. I'm guessing Charley himself is the thief."

"I'd never say that," Henry said.

"Why not?"

"Charley might be lying, but there's no profit in getting other people in trouble. Those things can come back to haunt you."

"Not even to protect yourself?"

"I didn't do anything wrong, and people will see that. I don't want to come out the other end smelling dirty just because I got someone else in trouble."

— 36 —

Henry sat on a knotty pinewood chair in the jailhouse on Hudson Street. In front of him were the jail cells with iron bars that had been built only few months earlier. The new cells replaced the shoddy rooms in the courthouse basement that previously held the town's prisoners. Henry had not seen the new cells before this day, but had long heard that the town's jail was the most secure in the territory.

Sheriff McIntosh pressured Henry over an hour for a confession that never came, asking him the same questions over and over. To Henry, every question seemed stained with an assumption of his guilt. He had committed no crime, but nothing he said seemed to make any difference. A fifteen-year-old orphan like him had no credibility against the accusations of businessmen like Isaac Stevens, David Abraham, and Matt Derbyshire.

"If you didn't take the money, who did?" McIntosh asked.

"I have no idea." Henry repeated the same answer every time the question was asked. He would never tell the sheriff — or anyone else — about the late night visit he received from Charley and Harry. He could not care less about Charley, who he no longer considered a friend, but he owed much to Harry's father. He didn't want anyone to know that Harvey Whitehill's own son and nephew were thieves.

"This town doesn't need wild boys like you causing trouble," the sheriff said, hollering at Henry. "I'll be watching you like a sharp-eyed eagle, and if I catch you breaking any of this town's laws, I'll make you wish you'd never been born. Do you understand what I'm saying?"

"Yes, sir." Henry knew that he didn't deserve the yelling, and if his mother hadn't taught him good manners, he would have told the sheriff to go to hell.

With no evidence against him other than Charley Stevens' accusations, the sheriff finally let him go. He then left the jailhouse and walked into a town that had been convinced he was a thief. The good citizens of the town wanted *someone* to pay for the crimes, and once the allegations against him had infected their thinking, he seemed unable to purge the falsehoods from their heads. Snide comments and indicting looks followed him everywhere he went.

Even Mr. Knight joined the chorus of people attacking his character. After returning to town and hearing the accusations against Henry, Mr. Knight dismissed Henry from the job that he had always performed as asked. Rather than expressing gratitude for keeping the meat market safe at night, Mr. Knight carried on about his regrets over hiring a thief like Henry in the first place. Mr. Knight told everyone that Henry could not be trusted.

A group of concerned citizens approached Gerald Truesdell and demanded that he not let Henry work at the Exchange any longer. Gerald wouldn't consider it. "He's a good worker and an honest boy," Gerald said. Despite Gerald's good reputation, his testimonials made no difference in changing people's perception of Henry as a thief.

"Nothing is more difficult to cure than a diseased imagination," his mother had once told him, and he was learning how right she had been.

The worst outcome of the false accusations came from David Abraham, who prohibited Henry from talking to Sarah.

"Father doesn't think I should talk with you any more," Sarah told Henry at school. "He said that if I was seen with you, it would give me a bad reputation. He said you can't be trusted."

"Do you believe that?" Henry asked.

"Of course not. I know you better than most people. I know what they're saying is not true, and if you give it time, I think people will begin to see you as I do."

"I hope so, but I'm beginning to wonder."

"Give it time," Sarah said.

"I still want to spend time with you, no matter what your father says. Will you be going to the dances at McGary's with your brother?"

"Yes, whenever I can."

"Would you be willing to meet me outside, in back of the dance hall, behind the Keystone Hotel? No one will see us."

"I will do that," Sarah said, putting her hand on his. "But don't talk to me at school, or Father will hear about it."

"What a mare's nest of problems, and I didn't do anything wrong."

"Just wait. People's suspicions will go away. I'm sure it won't last long."

Henry hoped Sarah was right.

— 37 —

Henry was walking down Broadway on his way to the Exchange when the water flowing down Main Street blocked him from crossing the street. He was standing near Bailey's Drug Store, an establishment sitting cater-cornered from the cabin where he had once lived with his mother. A late winter cloudburst had flooded the street, and as Henry stood outside the drug store looking for a way to get across, he spotted Harry Whitehill in front of the post office. Harry was examining the water at his feet, looking like he also wanted to cross the street.

It was the first time Henry had seen Harry outside of school since the town's merchants had come to their misguided conclusions about his thievery. He had thought about confronting Harry at school, but he respected Miss Richards too much to cause an incident in her presence. Now, in a place far removed from Miss Richards' classroom, his anger got the best of him.

Without saying a word he walked up to Harry and shoved him with all his strength. "You son-of-a-bitch. You could get me out of this mess. Why are you leaving me to hang?" His lip quivered from the frustration of dealing with all the false accusations that had been thrown at him.

"Don't get so hell-fired angry," Harry said, looking away from Henry toward the people standing outside Bailey's.

After Harry turned back to look at Henry, Henry rammed the palm of his hand into the underside of Harry's chin, causing Harry's head to bounce backward. Harry lost his balance and fell down, giving Henry an opportunity to kick him with the full force of his foot. As Harry rolled over, moaning and trying to avoid another kick in the ribs, he found himself lying face down in the water that was gushing through the street. Henry jumped on Harry's back and shoved his head into the water. Harry kicked and squirmed, unable to get free of Henry's grasp. If not for two men running out of Bailey's and pulling Henry off Harry's back, Harry might have drowned. The two men then wrestled Henry to the ground and held him down as he twisted and contorted his body, trying to break free.

"Calm down, son. CALM DOWN!" The men pinning Henry to the ground repeated their commands several times as Henry cussed and squirmed.

Within a few minutes, Sheriff McIntosh arrived. "The boy is out of control," one of the men said as the sheriff pulled a piece a rope from his belt to tie Henry's hands together. Henry was still on the ground as the two men holding him struggled to keep him motionless long enough for the sheriff to finish tying a knot behind his back.

"Get on home, Harry," the sheriff said, securing the rope around Henry's wrists. "The rest of you get moving, too. The fight's over, and I'll take care of everything from here."

The sheriff pulled Henry up and with a slap to the back of his head, began escorting him down the street with his hands tied behind his back.

The sheriff's sack suit looked as if it had just been cleaned and pressed stiff. His boots looked newly polished. Henry, who was wet, muddy, and angry, considered running away, figuring the sheriff, who was dressed to the hilt, would never catch him. But Henry's good sense told him not to run from a man with a loaded gun, a man who had the license of the law to protect his actions. Besides, he did not know where he would go. Everyone in Silver City knew him well enough that he wouldn't be able to hide very long.

"We'll get to my office and straighten this out," McIntosh said, again slapping Henry in the back of the head. "You better have a good story to justify what you just did to that boy. You could have drowned him."

At the jailhouse, McIntosh forced Henry onto the same uncomfortable pinewood chair where he had sat for his last interrogation. Henry's hands remained tied behind his back. McIntosh, saying nothing, wrapped a rope around Henry's chest, securing him tightly to the chair. The sheriff then left the room, leaving Henry alone for over an hour.

— 38 —

"What the hell were you doing?" McIntosh said when he returned to Henry. "Do you know the trouble you'd be in if Harry had drowned?"

"None of this is your business," Henry said.

"It sure as hell is!" the sheriff said, raising his voice. "When you almost kill someone, it's the law's business."

Henry didn't respond.

"You need to tell me what's going on between you and Harry?"

"I'm a talker, sheriff, but not on some issues."

McIntosh sat in a chair across from Henry, his hands on his knees. "Does Harry Whitehill know something about the stealing you've been blamed for?"

Henry said nothing.

"Why don't you just tell the truth? Get yourself out of trouble."

Again, Henry said nothing.

"I know your story," McIntosh said, "I know about your mama. It's hard to lose your mama, no matter what age. Some people tell me you're a good boy. Miss Richards tells me you're quick to help her around the schoolhouse and that you're good at your studies."

Henry looked to the side, determined to avoid eye contact with the sheriff.

"Gerald Truesdell tells me you've been no trouble living in his home. He said you always show up for work and you do a good job. Mrs. Truesdell tells me you're well mannered. I talked to Harvey Whitehill last week, and he told me you're a fine young man. He said your mama raised a good boy."

With his hands tied, Henry was unable to wipe the tears rolling down his cheeks.

"I've got an instinct that you're not the thief they say you are," McIntosh said.

Henry looked down, not wanting the sheriff to see the moisture in his eyes.

"Sizing up what you just did, I'd bet my grandmother's house that Harry Whitehill knows something about what's been going on. The way you attacked him, I figure he's either the one that got you into trouble or the one that could get you out of trouble."

Henry looked directly at McIntosh, tears staining his cheeks.

"I'm guessing that you're the type of boy who wouldn't say anything to get a friend in trouble, and I heard that Harry's your friend. I'm also guessing that you're the type of boy who would just as soon take care of a situation yourself rather than turn it over to someone else."

The sheriff stood up and walked toward Henry to remove the rope holding him to the chair. The sheriff then untied Henry's hands, freeing him to dry his cheeks.

"I suppose there's no sense in punishing a boy for just taking care of himself," McIntosh said.

Henry still had nothing to say.

"If I ever again hear of you fighting or trying to hurt someone, I'll lock you up. Do you understand that?"

"I understand," Henry said.

"Goddamn it!" McIntosh said, raising his voice again. "You're a slippery young fella to figure out. This is how our last meeting ended, and I'm not convinced you won't be back. Why the hell I'm letting you go, I don't know, especially after you almost drowned a boy."

"Maybe it's my good looks," Henry said, his buckteeth exaggerating the smile on his face.

McIntosh laughed at Henry's remark. "I've got a good reason to lock you up, but I can't help thinking there's more to this than you're willing to tell. I got a feeling you was justified in what you did to Harry. Letting you go won't make me look good, but I'll just prepare myself for the controversy. When did Gerald want you at the Exchange?"

"I'm already late."

"Well, you better get going. For my sake, you better stay out of trouble."

"You've got my word," Henry said.

— 39 —

On the nights Henry wasn't working, he stood behind the Keystone Hotel waiting for Sarah to arrive at McGary's. Whenever she came to the dance hall, her father and stepmother were with her, and Henry had to move into the shadows to avoid being seen. So far, he had obeyed Mr. Abraham's edict to stay away from Sarah. For over a month, he had not talked with her. He knew, however, that if he showed up enough times outside McGary's he would eventually catch her alone. She had, after all, promised to meet with him behind the hotel across from McGary's.

One Sunday evening, as he watched families enter through the rear door of the dance hall, he thought about the music coming from inside and how it reminded him of the time he had spent dancing with his mother. He missed his mother almost more than he could bear, and he wanted her alive again. He wanted one more night at McGary's with her — one more dance. He wanted enough time to tell her how much she had meant to him.

As he stood alone that night, listening to the music and thinking about his mother, he caught sight of Sarah and her brother Louis turning the corner from Yankie Street. As usual, he moved into the shadows. But when he noticed their father and stepmother were not with them, he stepped forward and whistled.

"Never say I'm not your friend," Louis said, catching sight of Henry next to the rear door of the Keystone. "I used all the poetry I could muster to persuade my father to let me and Sarah come here without him."

"It appears I now owe you two favors," Henry said, referring to the one favor he already owed Louis for helping him smoke Chauncey out of the privy.

"Father let us come alone as long as I promised I'd watch out for my sister," Louis said.

"She's safe with me," Henry said, smiling.

"No doubt," Louis said, as he left Henry and Sarah alone and walked into the dance hall. "You two enjoy your visit."

Henry took Sarah's hand and walked her toward a woodpile in a dark area behind the Keystone. He then sat next to her on a log that had not yet been split for firewood.

"No one should see us here," he told her.

Before he could say another word, she kissed him gently on the cheek. "I've missed you," she said.

"And I've missed you."

"Father told me that your attack on Harry was more evidence that I should stay away from you. He said you were born a troublemaker."

"Do you agree with him?"

"Not at all. I'm guessing Harry is the thief that people think you are."

"What makes you say that?"

"He's been bragging at school about some of the things he and Charley have been doing. They've never admitted stealing anything or doing anything against the law, but everyone can tell they've been doing some things they shouldn't."

"And you think he and Charley have been stealing?"

"He must be involved in some way. I know no other reason you would do what you did to him. I know you wouldn't steal, and I know you wouldn't attack someone without reason."

Henry was unable to keep the story to himself any longer and told Sarah everything that had happened. He began with the night Harry and Charley paid him a visit and ended with the day the sheriff decided not to lock him in a jail cell.

"The worst part is having everyone look at me with suspicion," he said.

"It's only a matter of time before the suspicion goes away," Sarah told him. "Everything will eventually die down and people will start seeing you for who you really are."

"Even your father?"

"Even my father. I've told him what I've heard, and he knows what I think."

"What has he said?"

"He thinks I've figured everything out wrong, blaming it on what he calls a 'mindless infatuation.' But I do think I've planted some doubt in what he's been hearing. Give him time and he'll join the Truesdells in defending you. I'm sure of that."

"What makes you so sure?"

"Give people time to learn about you and get to know you. They'll see who you really are. You're no thief."

"I heard I've lost Mr. Whitehill's support. Understandable, I suppose, considering I attacked his son."

"Just give everyone time. The truth will come out. People will someday be electing you to be the mayor of this town."

Henry laughed and pressed Sarah's hand into his. "I've missed talking with you," he said.

The two then sat quietly, holding hands, listening to the music coming from McGary's.

"I have a piano piece I want to play for you," Sarah said, breaking the silence. "It's a piece by Chopin that I learned last week. It's titled *Nocturne in E-flat*. I think about you every time I play it."

"I hope it's a cheerful tune," Henry said, smiling.

As the music from McGary's penetrated the cold night air, Henry inched closer to Sarah. "They're playing *Silver Threads*," he said. "You taught me that song, and I sang it to my Mam when she was sick."

"Would you like to dance?" Sarah asked.

"I haven't danced with anyone since I danced with my Mam."

Henry and Sarah held each other close as they swayed back and forth in the dark alley. Hidden from the people walking through the doors of McGary's, they listened to *Silver Threads Among the Gold*, moving back and forth to the rhythm of the melody, singing softly to each other as they danced.

> *"Yes, my darling, you will be*
> *Always young and fair to me."*

July 1875

Sarah, like Catherine, died early in the morning. When she took her last breath the sun was rising over the horizon to begin another day and bring Silver City to life. She died on a Sunday and was placed in the ground on Monday.

"It was the fever," Louis told Henry. "Mrs. Truesdell thinks it was typhoid that killed her. She got sick, and she just died."

Henry had not spent time alone with Sarah since four months earlier when he had danced with her behind the Keystone Hotel. Louis had tried to bring them together several other times, but failed due to his father's determination to keep her away from Henry. Louis told Henry that during the last weeks of Sarah's life, a time when school was out of session for the summer, she did little more than read and play the piano at home.

She now lay in a pine box placed next to a six-foot hole in the ground, killed by an illness that held no respect for youth. Her grave had been dug only a few feet from where Henry's mother was buried.

At first, Henry was reluctant to attend the funeral. He felt he would be unwelcome. He also felt uneasy about seeing Sarah's open casket, wishing he had never seen his mother in her pine box. He decided to attend the burial only after Louis asked him. Louis was his friend and had said that viewing the corpse was contrary to the Abraham's religious beliefs. Henry would therefore be able to remember Sarah as he last saw her.

Henry stood next to Louis at the burial, catching sight of the vacant look in his friend's eyes, a look that revealed the grief that Henry knew well. All he knew to do was put his hand on Louis' shoulder. He did not know what to say. In some situations it was better to say nothing, he figured.

After David Abraham, Sarah's father, read a few prayers, Sarah's body was lowered into the ground. Sarah's stepmother wept as Mr. Abraham then said a few words about how special his daughter had been and how hard it would be to live without her. He ended by reading from *Romeo and Juliet*, a play Sarah had been reading a few days before she fell ill.

> *"One poor and loving child,*
> *One thing to rejoice and solace in,*
> *And cruel death hath catch'd it from my sight!*
> *O woe! O woful, woful, woful day!"*

Overcome with emotion, Mr. Abraham looked up and said, "Well, friends, my girl is gone — she is actually gone."

The anger Henry had felt for being kept away from Sarah vanished in the presence of Mr. Abraham's grief. Henry knew what it felt like to lose someone he loved, and he did not wish that feeling on anyone.

Those who attended the burial took turns shoveling soil into Sarah's grave. The graveyard turned silent as the mourners then walked away and returned to town for a reception at the Abraham's home. Henry remained at Sarah's grave, standing next to Louis, who had not wanted to leave.

"I can't tell you how much I'll miss her," Louis said.

Henry knew that words of sympathy would do nothing to diminish his friend's pain. What could anyone say that would make a difference on a day like this?

"I may never be able to listen to anyone play the piano again," Louis said.

"That's not true," Henry said. "You'll want to listen to the piano every day. You'll want to think about Sarah every day."

Louis nodded. "I hope you're right."

Henry turned to look at the wooden marker on his mother's grave. "Mr. Derbyshire got my mother's name wrong. He spelled Catherine with a K, when it should be a C. Make certain Mr. Derbyshire gets Sarah's name right. Make sure he puts the h at the end of her name."

Henry did not go to the reception that afternoon. He knew what Mr. Abraham thought of him and realized a boy with his reputation would not be welcome in the Abraham home. Alone with his thoughts, he took a long walk past Hudson Street to a hill east of town where he sat until after sunset. As he sat on the hill he looked down on the Legal Tender Corral directly in front of him and the jailhouse next to it. He then looked up at the scores of lights beyond the jailhouse glowing from the lanterns of Silver City. Only a few months earlier the town had looked so different to him. He had enjoyed living in Silver City when his mother was alive, when he could talk with Sarah. At one time he was known as Catherine's son, a well-mannered boy who enjoyed singing and dancing at McGary's. He was now a thief, a boy not to be trusted.

He had lost so much in only one year.

— 41 —

Suspicions about Henry's guilt would not go away. It had been five months since the nighttime theft of five dollars and two bottles of whiskey from Matt Derbyshire. Henry had been accused of that crime and many others. Wherever he went he carried the burden of his tarnished reputation. Store clerks watched him with distrustful eyes, and whenever something was missing, people were quick to suspect that he had stolen it.

Over the months, he continued to proclaim his innocence to anyone who would listen. He had never stolen anything and had nothing to hide. But the truth seemed unimportant to the people who had already formed an opinion about him. The word "thief" had been carved onto his reputation, and he was learning that it would not easily be removed.

He had even lost the support of Harvey Whitehill, the man who had once done so much to help him. Harvey did not like what Henry had done to his son Harry and had begun criticizing Henry in public.

"That boy's a born criminal," Harvey said one night at the Exchange. When Harvey spoke those words he was pointing at Henry and talking loud enough that the words thundered across the barroom. "The boy can't be trusted. I'd no more trust him than I'd trust a rabid dog."

Henry was determined not to tell the story that might help clear his name. He would not tell how Harvey's son and nephew were the real thieves. Even if he had told others what happened, the truth would have fallen on ears unwilling to hear what he was saying. Too much time had passed, and the story, although true, would sound like nothing more than the desperate tale of a boy trying to get out of trouble.

Henry had decided to follow Sarah's advice and give his accusers time to see that he was no thief. He had no other choice. He would stay out of trouble, go to school, and work hard at the hotel. He would regain everyone's trust no matter how long it took. Above all, he wanted to regain Harvey's trust.

Harvey had been elected sheriff in April after Charlie McIntosh left town. Before leaving, McIntosh had said he wanted compensation from the town council for taking a bullet in his leg while he was making an arrest. After his request was denied, he took $3000 from the town's funds and left Silver City. Most people believed he had gone to Mexico.

Henry missed having McIntosh as sheriff. McIntosh had not believed he was a thief and thought he was justified in attacking Harry. With McIntosh as sheriff, Henry at least had the law on his side.

"There's no proof the boy's a thief," McIntosh had told those who wanted Henry locked in a jail cell. "I won't punish a boy just for standing up for himself."

Now, with Harvey serving as sheriff, Silver City had a lawman determined to set Henry straight.

Henry first faced Harvey's prejudice the day a rancher named Abel Webb came into town to buy cooking supplies for his wife. When Abel entered Bailey's Drug Store he left his buckboard unattended in the street and a keg of butter disappeared from the back of his wagon.

Harvey never found a witness to the crime, although Henry had been seen walking east on Broadway about the same time Abel said the butter was stolen. Henry was only heading toward his job at the hotel, but that made no difference to Harvey. After the keg of butter was found in the alley behind the Exchange, Harvey just assumed Henry was responsible.

Harvey pulled Henry away from work that evening and walked him to the jailhouse for questioning. Harvey treated Henry as if he had committed a crime worthy of territorial prison. Henry tried to defend himself, but Harvey wouldn't listen, interrupting everything Henry said with a tongue-lashing that Henry didn't deserve.

"When I find proof about what you've been doing, I'll lock you up," Harvey said. "Your mother would be ashamed of you. She would never have believed that she could raise a boy who belongs behind bars, and I'm damn sure going to put you there the first chance I get."

After a scolding that lasted almost longer than Henry could stand, Harvey let Henry return to work. Henry walked back to the Exchange that night alarmed by Harvey's unwillingness even to listen, aware that Silver City now had a sheriff who would never believe anything he said. Henry wondered whether he should leave town, but did not know where he would go or what he would do to support himself if he left. He was only fifteen years old and had often been told he looked much younger. He wondered if anyone other than Gerald Truesdell would ever give him a job.

— 42 —

A few people still defended Henry. Louis and Chauncey remained his loyal friends. Even Harry had forgiven him.

"I guess I had it coming," Harry told Henry one day at school.

"I'm sorry about what I did. I hope you'll forgive me for not coming clean to my father about why you attacked me."

Henry accepted Harry's apology with a halfhearted handshake. He had gone out of his way to keep Harry's wrongdoing to himself, but Harry seemed to have no desire to do something that would clear his reputation. At least Harry was good enough to apologize, unlike Charley Stevens, who simply avoided Henry.

The Truesdells also continued to support Henry. "I can't imagine that Catherine McCarty's son would ever steal anything," Clara told Henry. "I'm not sure why you attacked Harvey's boy, but I'm certain you had your reasons. I promised your mother I would take care of you, and I won't break that promise. I also promised her I'd take care of Josie, and from what I've heard, he's doing just fine with the Dyers."

Henry had been too busy to keep abreast of everything his brother was doing. According to what Clara and others had told him, Josie was still working at the Orleans Club, doing everything Mr. Dyer asked of him. Henry had no idea whether Josie had heard that his own brother was a thief. But with the entire town talking about it, Henry didn't know how Josie would have avoided the stories. He hoped Josie believed the accusations were false. If not, he'd set him straight one day.

Gerald Truesdell, like Sheriff McIntosh, had figured out the reason that Henry attacked Harry Whitehill.

"I figure Harry had something to do with the thievery they're blaming on you," Gerald told Henry. "I figure you had grounds for what you did, and you won't get any criticism from me."

Henry appreciated the Truesdells' support and was grateful for everything they had done for him. Even so, he didn't how much longer he could remain in their home.

Unknown to anyone in town other than Henry and the Truesdell boys, Gerald and Clara did not get along and argued endlessly. Henry assumed they no longer loved each other — if they ever had. They certainly never showed any fondness for each other.

Clara was the only person in town with training as a nurse, and Gerald thought she spent too much time away from home. Clara told Gerald she was taking care of the sick and saw no reason to remain at home when he spent all his time running the Exchange.

To Henry, the disagreements and the yelling made little sense. All he knew for certain was the Truesdell home had turned into an unpleasant place to live. With every argument he felt he was witness to a secret that should only be known to people in the Truesdell family. He was not a member of the family and needed to move out.

To avoid returning to the Truesdells' home, Henry began spending time after work in the cantinas on Chihuahua Hill. After seeing what whiskey had done to Bill Antrim, he had no desire to drink the tequila or any other alcohol served in the cantinas. He had, however, developed a taste for the chile peppers dished up with the hot tortillas and frijoles. He also enjoyed attending the bailes, the dances he wished his mother had seen before she died. She would have loved the liveliness of the music and the spirit of fun on the dance floor.

His favorite cantina was the one called La Sala, a place with a large dance hall where spectators took seats on both sides as they listened to music and watched dancers change partners. Most of the spectators were mothers or grandmothers hoping to see young señoritas find a husband.

As the weather grew warmer, Henry began spending his nights

in an abandoned shack located at the top of Chihuahua Hill. The shack had once belonged to a Chinaman named Sam Chung and would have still been occupied by Sam had the Mexicans on the Hill not turned against him because he was Chinese. As far as Henry could tell, Sam had done nothing to deserve banishment from the Hill. He had simply paid a price for something his employer had done, something that intensified the prejudice against all Chinese residents of the town.

Sam worked for Charlie Sun, a man who married a Mexican woman. Henry figured Charlie would have married a Chinese woman if one had been available, but none had yet moved to Silver City. When his wife became pregnant, he bought drinks one night for everyone at La Sala. "Drink to me," Charlie said flashing a big smile at the recipients of the free tequila. "My child will bring the Chinese and Mexicans in this town together."

When the baby was born and Charlie saw that its skin was dark, he changed his tune. "No nigger babies in my home," he told his wife. He then took the newborn child behind his house and threw it in the mud with an old sow. The sow trampled the baby to death before Charlie's wife could save it. Charlie would have probably then killed his own wife, but a couple of Mexican ranch hands that lived on the Hill saw what was happening and pulled her away from the scene.

To the people on the Hill, Charlie Sun's infanticide was the only evidence they needed to confirm their low opinion of the Chinese living in Silver City. Sam Chung was banished from his shack on the Hill. Henry couldn't understand why Sam should pay a price for a crime committed by someone else. Even so, he had no qualms about moving into Sam's shack and getting away from the Truesdells' quarreling.

Henry's life on the Hill was made easier by the ease with which he picked up Spanish. He had a good ear for the language, and after only a few weeks on the Hill, he was able to include himself in conversations on almost any topic.

"I must have Mexican blood in my Irish family," he told his friends at La Sala. "Give me time and people might mistake me for a Mexican."

Henry enjoyed the festive dancing and singing in the cantinas and found the lighthearted atmosphere much different from what he had seen at McGary's.

"The people on the Hill seem more unbuttoned than the people I saw dancing at McGary's," he once told a señorita during a dance. "I think there's more fun up here than on Main Street."

"God blesses those who are not greedy," replied the girl. "And there is certainly less greed on the Hill than on Main Street."

"The folks on Main Street have much to learn from all of you," Henry said. He then leaned forward to kiss the señorita, a kiss that prompted a vigorous ovation from an old man sitting at the bar.

"My name is Abelardo Cisneros, and I like you," said the old man after Henry finished the dance. "They tell me you're a thief, but I've always liked thieves as long as they steal from the right people. Come and join me."

Unlike most people in the cantina, Abelardo did not seem drunk. His broad smile and clear eyes caught Henry's attention more than the drooping white mustache and wrinkled skin that revealed his advanced age. He wore a red and black sombrero with a wide rim. Henry joined him at the bar and felt the welcoming spirit of a lonely old man needing someone to hear his gray-haired wisdom.

"That señorita has eyes for you," Abelardo told Henry. "I think you should do more than kiss her."

Henry laughed and put his hand on Abelardo's shoulder. "She's too good for me. She has no need to fish in my troubled waters."

"What troubles you?" Abelardo asked.

"On Main Street they say I'm no good — but we should talk about something else."

"No," Abelardo said, smiling. "I want to hear about Main Street. On the Hill, we build with adobe, the way people have been building forever in this part of the world. On Main Street, they build with red bricks, which is just another way of showing off. Too much money on Main Street. Too much interest in the things that don't matter. If you've been stealing from those American *pendejos*, you've only been giving them what they deserve."

Henry understood the point Abelardo was making and nodded in agreement.

"You might be right, considering the way I've been treated down there. They think I'm a thief, and they've got it all wrong. I'm just trying to take care of myself and do the right thing. But some of those *pendejos* that you are talking about are sure making it hard for me to stay on the right side of things."

"What's right depends on who's got the money, wouldn't you agree?" Abelardo said.

"I guess so," Henry said. "I guess so."

— 43 —

It wasn't long before Henry began looking for a way to move

out of his shack on the Hill. The rotten planks of wood and crooked construction did not protect him from the summer rainstorms that flooded the flimsy structure. Unless he wanted to continue sleeping in pools of water, he needed to find other lodgings.

He heard from a miner at the Exchange that Sarah Brown had a room available at her boarding house. He had thought he didn't have enough money to rent his own room, but his hopes rose when he heard how much she charged. He could afford what she wanted and decided to ask whether she would take him in.

Mrs. Brown was a dour woman who had been widowed by a mining accident west of town. Henry knew Mrs. Brown had caused his mother much aggravation at meetings of the Ladies Educational Society, and he had never been able to look at Mrs. Brown without thinking of the stories his mother had told him. According to his mother, Mrs. Brown possessed a small-minded fear of children playing in the street. Henry had always thought that her unsightly appearance matched what he had been told about her personality. Her face seemed fixed in a permanent scowl that told Henry she didn't trust very many people, if any.

Mrs. Brown depended on rent payments from her boarders for a livelihood. Even so, she told Henry she was reluctant to give him a room.

"I've heard you're the type I'll need to keep my eye on," she told him. "I can't let you stay with me unless you refuse to touch anything in my home other than what's in your room."

"I'm as honest as I can be," Henry said. "You can trust me to do whatever you ask. If you talk with Mrs. Truesdell or my teacher Miss Richards, they'll tell you I'm reliable."

"I've already heard all that I want to know about you," Mrs.

Brown said with a sneer. "They tell me you're a charmer, but you can't charm me."

"All I can say is that you can trust me. I've got a job with Mr. Truesdell at the Exchange. I can pay you a dollar and a quarter every week."

"It goes against my better judgment, but I hate to leave a room empty. Maybe there's nothing wrong with you that a Christian home can't cure."

"You have no need to worry," Henry said.

"I knew your mother, and I just met your stepfather. I'm certain her attentive ghost and his proximity can be used to keep you straight."

Henry did not like Mrs. Brown talking about his mother's ghost, but decided to ignore the comment. He was, however, curious how Mrs. Brown knew Bill, whom he had not seen for six months.

"When did you meet my stepfather?" Henry asked.

"He was here two weeks ago. Stayed in the same room I'm giving you. I just assumed he was the one who told you to see me."

"No ma'am. I didn't even know he was in town."

"He was here, but he's already left. He told me he was going to Clifton. I have no misgivings about contacting him if you cause me any trouble. Your mother couldn't keep you traveling straight, but I'm certain the Christian guidance I can give you will keep you on the right path."

Henry disliked Mrs. Brown even more with every word she spoke. But his good manners, as well as his desire for a room that would keep him dry, kept him from telling her that she should keep her Christian guidance to herself. There was nothing he could learn from her that would improve on anything his mother had taught him.

"Do you know why my stepfather was here?" Henry asked.

"He said he had banking business to attend to. That's all I know."

Probably taking more of Mam's money for his prospecting schemes, Henry thought.

"I'll have your room ready tomorrow," Mrs. Brown said. "I need to do a little cleaning before you move in."

"Thank you," Henry said. "I'll drop off my belongings before I go to the Exchange."

Henry hoped he wouldn't be staying long with Mrs. Brown. At the first opportunity, he would find somewhere else to live and get away from her pig-faced grumpiness.

— 44 —

"I heard your stepfather was back in town," Gerald told Henry at the Exchange that evening.

"Do you know if he's still here?" Henry asked.

"I don't think so. Isaac Stevens told me he's already left for Arizona. It sounds like he didn't pay you a visit."

"I never saw him, but I doubt he had any desire to see me."

"I heard he went to see Isaac and then left town with the money Isaac had invested for him. You can tell me if it's none of my business, but where'd he get that money? I heard it was a fair amount he took from Isaac."

"Some of it was his. Some of it was Mam's. She made money running a laundry in Wichita, and Bill gave her money to Mr. Stevens after we moved here."

"Seems like you should have talked to Isaac about that money. If it was your mama's money, at least some of it should have gone to you and Josie."

"It's too late now. Besides, Mr. Stevens is part of the crowd that won't have anything to do with me. He's convinced I led his son astray. He badmouths me to everyone."

"I could talk to him in your favor."

"Like I said. It's too late now. It appears my Mam's money has gone to Arizona."

Henry knew that even if he had talked to Isaac about his mother's money, it would have done no good. The money was in Bill's name, and according to Bill, neither Henry nor Josie had a legal claim to it.

As Henry served food and drinks at the hotel that night, he thought about how he should at least try and take some of that money away from Bill. Bill owed him and Josie what their mother could no longer provide, and it was time that someone persuaded that bastard to pay. Maybe another knife at Bill's throat would be all the persuading he needed. Henry hoped Josie would help him find Bill and take what was rightfully theirs. He would find Josie and ask him to help. If Josie refused, Henry would do it on his own.

— 45 —

Henry set out to find Josie by going first to the Dyers' home and asking Mrs. Dyer about his brother's whereabouts. She told him to go to the Orleans Club, and when he arrived at the Orleans Club a bartender directed him to the rooms behind the saloon. In one of those rooms he discovered Josie sitting on a broken-down cot, looking relaxed and too drained of energy to stand up. Josie's eyes were washed out, and a foot-long opium pipe rested beside him on the cot.

"Goddammit, Josie," Henry said. "What the hell are you doing?"

Josie looked at Henry and seemed confused, unable to understand what his brother was saying. Henry snatched the pipe from next to Josie and threw it to the floor.

"This would not have happened if Mam was alive," Henry said.

Josie did not respond, and Henry knew it was a waste of time to talk with his brother until the effects of the opium wore off. Trembling with anger, Henry walked back to the saloon at the front of the Orleans Club. Joe Dyer should have kept watch over his brother, and Joe needed to pay a price for his slapdash guardianship.

As Henry entered the saloon, he spotted Joe standing next to the bar, his back to the doorway Henry had just entered. Henry walked toward Joe, grabbing an empty bottle of redeye from a table as he moved toward him. Then, using all the force he could muster from his right arm, he landed a sharp blow to the side of Joe's head. Joe fell to the floor like he had been dropped from a second-story window.

"My brother's only twelve years old, and you were supposed to take care of —"

Before Henry could finish, two ruffians who worked at the Orleans Club grabbed him and threw him to the ground. Dropping to the floor, the two men pinned Henry's arms and legs under the weight of their bodies and held Henry motionless, not a difficult task considering his small frame. The two men then gazed at Joe, acting as if they were waiting for instructions about what to do next.

Joe, looking stunned, pulled himself up from the floor and

stumbled toward Henry. He then stomped on Henry's head with the heel of his boot.

"Goddamned wild-assed kid," Joe said. "They've said you're no good."

Henry struggled to break free but remained in the tight grip of the two men holding him.

"Keep my brother away from your poison," Henry said through clenched teeth.

"Shit, kid," Joe said. "What are you upset about? That Antrim boy never causes me any trouble."

"He's lying in an opium den in the back of your saloon."

"I have no problem with that, and it shouldn't matter to you what he does on his own time."

At Joe's instructions, the two men pulled Henry up, continuing to hold him tight enough that he would not attack Joe.

Joe put a hand on the side of his head where Henry had hit him. He appeared dazed as he examined Henry.

"Look at you," Joe said. "You're a runty little fella, and you're certainly not worth my time." Joe motioned the two men to take Henry outside.

After Henry was escorted to the batwing doors of the Orleans Club, he turned to look at Joe. "My brother's name is McCarty, not Antrim."

"That's news to me," Joe said, sounding uninterested. "I've been calling him Antrim since he started working for me, and he's never once protested."

Henry was thrown out of the Orleans Club into the mud on Main Street. Lying on his side and looking across the street, he saw the building that once held McGary's saloon and dance hall. It had recently been changed into a furniture factory. Farther down the street he spotted the cabin where he had once lived with his Mam, the place where she had died. A shoe repair sign hung over the door, above the spot where she once sold sweetcakes.

Henry had lost his mother only ten months earlier, but so much had changed. It seemed like years since she had passed away.

— 46 —

The spacious living quarters that were reserved for Mrs. Brown in her own home were kept clean and tidy. Her furniture was simple but elegant. The room she gave Henry, on the other hand, was no more than a cramped rectangular box at the back of the house — large enough for a bed and little else.

With four red bricks salvaged from a building site north of Broadway, Henry had propped the bed high enough to slide a trunk under it. The trunk contained his meager possessions: a blanket, a copy of *The Death of Arthur*, a few copies of *The Police Gazette*, and some old clothes.

The mattress was hard and lumpy, not worth the money he was paying Mrs. Brown and not much more comfortable than the dirt floor where he had slept in his shack on the Hill. At least rainwater wouldn't be soaking his bedding as it had on the Hill.

Henry, still in pain from Joe Dyer's kick to his head, found it difficult to fall asleep. Images of Josie in the opium den haunted him, and his mind raced with thoughts about what he might have done differently to help his brother. Even though talking to Josie usually accomplished about as much as a dog barking at a knot of wood, he wished he had done more to help his brother.

He also could not escape the images in his head of his mother and Sarah lying in their graves. They were gone forever, and he wondered whether he would ever break free of the loneliness he felt without them.

When he finally fell asleep he dreamed about Bill returning from a prospecting trip. In the dream, Bill was pleased to see Henry and invited him and Josie to dinner at the Exchange.

"I can see that you boys have been taking care of yourselves," Bill said. "I'm proud of you."

Bill then learned from Josie about a recent theatrical directed by Miss Richards, a show that had featured Henry as the Head Man.

"Henry's quite the theater man," Josie told Bill. "He's got a singing voice that makes old women cry, and his jokes make everyone laugh."

"Too bad your mama isn't around to see that," Bill said, "I can hear her laughing. You would have made your mother proud."

Henry then dreamed about Bill saying something that he would never hear when he was awake. "Your mama's money is safe with me. She made that money in Wichita, and it belongs to both of you. If you want, I can invest it in a business — maybe a meat market like the one I ran in Wichita. You two can come live with me. You can help me run the business."

Henry awoke the next morning, ending the make-believe world of his dreams. It was true that Miss Richards had directed a theatrical. She called it *The Histrionic*, and Henry had been the Head Man. But Josie, like Bill, never saw the show. Henry's audience-pleasing performance ended with him returning to his shack on the Hill. No more than an hour after the show, Henry had found himself alone, sleeping on the ground with desert mice crawling over him as rainwater seeped under the walls of his shack and puddled next to him.

The real world that Henry lived in was far removed from the one in his dreams.

August 1875

— 47 —

George Schaefer had been gone from Silver City for six months before returning and taking a room at Mrs. Brown's boarding house. Mrs. Brown put him in the room next to Henry's, and Henry watched with amusement as Mrs. Brown made George remove his turquoise and gold sombrero whenever he walked into her home. Every time George entered the house she reminded him to remove his hat, and every time she reminded him, he objected. He would then consent to her request after she threatened to send him somewhere else to live. Henry chuckled to himself at the predictability of their confrontations.

Henry had never before realized how much an article of clothing could mean to someone. George demanded that people call him Sombrero Jack, and Henry noticed a distinct change in George's personality when he wasn't wearing his sombrero. Without the hat, he would lift his shoulders high, acting like he wanted to cover his ears. He would look embarrassed and timid, physically smaller, with a spine that seemed bent. When he wore the hat, everything about him would change. His back would straighten and his shoulders relax. He would swagger about as if he owned every room he walked into.

Whether he was wearing the sombrero or not, Henry sensed trouble whenever George was around, and Henry didn't want much to do with him. He had heard too many stories about the mischief George could cause. But circumstances had placed them in the same boarding house in adjacent rooms, and Henry had no choice but to make the best of the situation. He couldn't avoid George and had no choice but trying to get along with him.

"Those Georgetown bosses were always after me," George told Henry one evening, explaining the reason he had moved back to Silver City. "Those sons-of-bitches never let up, blaming me for everything that went wrong. They said I was a thief."

Henry could have told the same story about himself.

George had been working in the mines at Georgetown, even though he claimed to be a stonemason. He told Henry that he had returned to Silver City hoping to find work in what he called "*this* rathole," rather than "*that* rathole."

"Maybe this rathole can give me some masonry work," George said. "I'm tired of those goddamned mines."

"Good luck," Henry said, wondering whether anyone would want to hire someone with George's way of thinking.

"Join me for some redeye at the Orleans Club," George said, poking his finger into Henry's chest as if he was demanding that Henry go with him.

"I have no interest in drinking at the Orleans Club," Henry said. He had learned from working at the Exchange that whiskey too often brought nothing but trouble to those who drank it.

"I might take your rejection as an insult," George said. "Come to the Orleans Club and we'll shake a new friendship out a bottle of whiskey."

Henry did not want to go to the Orleans Club but feared a refusal would only turn George against him. He certainly didn't need anyone else joining the number of people that were already out to get him.

"I guess I could use something to eat," Henry said, "but let's go to the Exchange. I don't think Mr. Dyer wants me in his place anymore."

"I knew you'd come around, and the Exchange is as good a place as any, I guess. Let me buy you a bowl of stew and you can wash it down with a shot of whiskey."

"Glass of water will be all I need."

"I never heard of anyone not wanting a shot of redeye. Is something wrong with you, Antrim?"

"My name's McCarty, and I've seen too many drunks at the Exchange. There's no need for me to join that organization."

"Your code's as twisted as your teeth. Next thing I know you'll be joining a church."

"I doubt that," Henry said. "If you want to drink the redeye, go ahead. I'm not the type to preach at others. Just trying to stay out of trouble, that's all."

— 48 —

Henry followed a step behind as George strutted down Main Street with his sombrero placed securely on his head,

"They say you're a thief," George said, turning to look at Henry, who was struggling to keep up with the pace. "They told me to watch my pockets when I'm around you, and I'd bet that's why Joe Dyer doesn't want you in the Orleans Club."

"I've never stole anything, and I could open my own business if I had a dollar for every time someone called me a thief."

"That's what I'd expect a thief to say."

"Just know that your pockets are safe around me," Henry said, as he followed George into the Exchange.

Finding a table next to the door, George motioned Henry to take a seat.

"Can I trust you with something?" George said.

"I suppose so," Henry said, feeling suspicious.

George whispered to Henry across the table. "I've got a plan to steal from a Chinaman."

Henry didn't respond and wasn't looking forward to the direction the conversation was going.

"That Chinaman Charlie Sun," George said, "the one that owns that laundry in hop town. No one cares if someone steals from that coolie."

"He might be a Chinaman, but he's got a right to what he earns," Henry said.

George looked over his shoulder to see if anyone was listening. "They say that Chinaman killed his own baby. Threw it to the pigs. I heard that no one in town said a damned thing, as if there was nothing unusual about a Chinaman killing a baby."

"I don't know much about that."

"Have you heard that Chinaman talk? He sounds like he was clubbed in the head when he was young. Said he was attacked by Indians once. 'They killa me fourteen times. They killa me fourteen times.' No one knows what the hell he's talking about. I've got no qualms about stealing from that rail hopper."

"That Chinaman's talk is odd," Henry admitted, "but that

doesn't mean someone should take his property. He worked for it just like anyone else."

"Come on, Antrim. Help me out. We'll make a little money for drinking and whoring."

"I don't drink, and I don't whore. And why do you keep calling my Antrim? My name's McCarty."

"No need to get so gusty. I knew your father in Georgetown and figured you had his name."

"Bill Antrim is not my father. Don't connect me to him. He doesn't support me, and I don't support him."

"You at least support your friends, I hope."

"I didn't know we were friends," Henry said. "As far as I'm concerned, we're just a couple fellows trying to get along."

George reached into his coat pocket and pulled out a six-inch derringer. "This is the type of gun Booth used to kill that traitor Lincoln. No need for me to worry about you being a traitor, I hope."

"I'm no thief, and I don't tell tales. Just trying to get along." Henry hoped his smile would lighten the mood.

"You're a likable fella, that's for sure." George said, placing the derringer back in his pocket. "Just keep what I've told you quiet or you'll find yourself with a bullet in your head like Dishonest Abe. If you hear that some Chinaman's been robbed, don't even wring your hands with regret."

"Wouldn't think of it," Henry said.

— 49 —

Miss Richards reached into a crate of new books and handed a stack to Henry. "You'll be one of the older students in this year's class," she said, motioning Henry to place the books on a shelf. She was organizing her classroom and had recruited Henry to help. "I have some good books for you this session. Charles Dickens. Samuel Clemens. Bret Harte. You couldn't ask for better books to read."

"If you say they're good, I'll trust you," Henry said. "You've never given me a book I didn't like." Henry enjoyed helping Miss Richards. She seemed to like him and always treated him with respect.

"I want you to read this book first," she said, handing Henry a copy of *The Luck of Roaring Camp*. "The main story is about a boy who brings good luck to a bad luck town."

"It's certainly not about me, is it?" Henry said, laughing.

"It's a fun book and should give you something to think about. It breaks my heart that Sarah won't be here to talk about these books with you. She loved to read."

Henry glanced up from the book and looked at Miss Richards. The expression on her face revealed a sincere concern for what he was feeling.

"Are you getting settled with what happened to Sarah?" she asked. "There's no embarrassment in feeling sad."

"I'm fine," Henry said. "Thank you for asking."

Miss Richards looked into Henry's eyes, and he looked away, feeling uncomfortable with her attempt to gauge his private grief.

"How long has it been since you've bought new clothes?" she asked. Henry was wearing his usual dirty leather vest, brown pants, and ragged checkered shirt. He had worn holes in his moccasins under the balls of his feet and, like the rest of his clothes, his moccasins were too small for comfort.

"These clothes used to belong to my brother. He's younger than me, but bigger. I've been wearing them since Mam died."

"That was a year ago. You're not a big boy, but you have grown in the last year and those clothes don't look like they fit you well. You should make a trip to Mr. Abraham's store and buy a new set. You should change everything, from your moccasins to your collar."

"I don't have the money, and if I did, I don't think Mr. Abraham would let me in his store."

"He will let you in if I'm with you, and I'll pay for the new clothes."

"I don't want any charity."

"I don't consider it charity. You've spent so much time helping me around the school, I'll consider it payment for your service."

Henry thought for a moment and decided to accept the offer. "Looser-fitting clothes would be more comfortable, I admit."

"Can we meet at the Abraham store next week on Friday afternoon?" Miss Richards asked. "About one o'clock."

Henry nodded. "I appreciate your kindness," he said.

"Forgive me for changing the subject," Miss Richards said, "but I heard that you are sharing a room with that boy who calls himself Sombrero Jack."

"We're both staying at Mrs. Brown's. We're not sharing a room."

"From what I hear, that boy is nothing but trouble. Mr. Truesdell is concerned about you spending too much time with him. Sheriff Whitehill told me the same thing, although he thinks you're already a troublemaker."

Henry winced at the reference to Harvey Whitehill, "I don't know what to do to set things right with that man," Henry said. "It seems nothing I do or say is acceptable to him."

Miss Richards tipped her head sideways and looked again into his eyes. "I can help you find a better place to live, someplace away from Sombrero Jack — and Mrs. Brown. I know Mrs. Brown from the Educational Society, and she's been convinced by Mr. Scott that boys your age are just no good. She's already convinced you're a thief."

"She's willing to take my money when I pay for her room."

"She's also prejudiced against you. But I mostly fear the trouble Sombrero Jack might pull you into. It might not take much more than an association with him to get yourself locked up."

"Thank you for wanting to help, but I can take care of myself."

"I still think you should find a better place to live. You're a good boy. You're well mannered, and you've done well in school. You've always been quick to do chores for me and help me whenever I needed it. I told Mrs. Brown all of that and she believed none of it. She's convinced that you're on your way to becoming an outlaw unless she does something to teach you a lesson. I don't think you should be living in her home."

"Give me time, and I'll show Mrs. Brown that I'm on a straight path. Mr. Whitehill, too. My Mam always told me that charm is stronger than beauty, and in my case that better be true. I'm not the prettiest flower in the pot, you know."

Miss Richards laughed. "From what I've heard, your mother was a good woman. I'm sure you miss her."

"I do." Henry grew silent for a moment. "I guess I should get going. Mr. Truesdell is expecting me at work."

"You'll meet me next Friday at Mr. Abraham's?"

"Yes, ma'am. I appreciate what you're doing."

Henry left Miss Richards that afternoon with a bounce in his step and high hopes that his bad luck was about to change. School would begin soon, and he would have a new set of clothes. He suspected that with a little more time he would be able to show everyone that he was no thief. His mother had told him that patient people received just rewards, and he was willing to be patient. With a teacher like Miss Richards helping him, he figured everything would eventually turn for the best.

— 50 —

Henry had placed the package George gave him in the trunk under his bed. The package was smaller than a butter churn, nothing more than a blanket wrapped around a few items. Henry had no idea what was in the package.

"I'm moving out," George had said. "I'm thinking about going back to Georgetown, but I'm not sure yet and need someone to hold this until I find out if I can get a job in the mines again. It seems no one wants to hire me as a stonemason in this town. If I don't come back, you can keep what you want."

Henry waited several days, and when George didn't return, he decided to unwrap the package. Inside, he found two revolvers and some men's clothing — shirts, trousers, and undergarments. The clothes were too large for Henry. They even appeared too large for George, who must have outweighed Henry by thirty pounds. Henry couldn't help but wonder whether the items had been stolen.

Henry decided to take the bundle of items to Harvey. If they were stolen, Harvey would need to know about it because he was the sheriff. If not, Harvey could hold the items until George returned. Besides, if Henry showed Harvey what George had given him, it might serve his reputation well. It just might be the first step in showing Harvey he could be trusted. A trip to the sheriff's office, however, would have to wait until later. Henry needed to get to work.

Henry wrapped the items in the blanket, returned the package to the trunk, and pushed it under the bed. He would show it to Harvey later.

September 1875

Harvey Whitehill had been patrolling Silver City's streets, stepping into one saloon at time, when he found trouble at the Orleans Club. After entering the saloon he saw a boy standing motionless, pinned against the wall, Joe Dyer's gun shoved behind the boy's right ear. The boy, only eighteen or nineteen years old, was cursing at Joe, showing everyone in the saloon that he had no more sense than a horse lubber. From what Harvey could tell, Joe was only a few seconds away from either striking the boy with the butt of the gun or putting a bullet through the back of the boy's head.

"There's no need to hurt that pisspot," Harvey said, speaking loud enough that he hoped to keep Joe from hurting the boy. "I'll take care of him from here."

It was early evening with still enough sunlight shining on the town that the lanterns of Main Street had not yet been lit. Harvey looked at the boy and figured he had been drinking all afternoon.

"He's so drunk he can't recognize a winning hand of faro when he sees it," Joe told Harvey. "He's been here all day, and lost all his money. I want him gone and he's refusing to leave."

"Come with me, and bring that goddamned hat with you," Harvey said, referring to the turquoise and gold sombrero the boy

173

was holding in his left hand. "It's better I throw you in a cell than watch Joe put a bullet through your head. Maybe a little time in jail will make you realize what a mother's jackass you are."

Patrons of the Orleans Club hooted and cheered with appreciation as Harvey escorted the boy out of the saloon.

"I know about you," Harvey said. "Your name's George Schaefer, and I've been told you're nothing but trouble." Harvey's gun was cocked and pointed at George's back as they walked toward the jailhouse. "From what I've heard, you wouldn't be welcome in any town."

"They call me Sombrero Jack," George said, slurring his words.

"I don't care if they call you Robert E. Lee," Harvey said. "In my book you amount to no more than the chicken shit I cleaned out of my hen house this morning."

After locking George in a jail cell, Harvey completed some paperwork for the territorial government. From behind the oak door that separated the cell from the sheriff's office, Harvey could hear George hollering and complaining with an intoxicated anger that filled the jailhouse with obscenities. Harvey ignored the rant until it was time to check the lock on George's cell and go home. Harvey was looking forward to putting the jailhouse in the hands of his deputy and getting a good night's sleep.

"Don't leave me in this cell all night," George said. "I need out. I can't stand it here."

"You'll calm down when the whiskey wears off," Harvey said. "I'll let you out tomorrow."

Harvey was walking away from George's cell, ready to go home, when George said something that made him pause.

"That Antrim kid should be in here not me," George bellowed.

"That kid shouldn't be roaming free."

"What are you saying, George?" Harvey asked, returning to the cell.

"Goddammit, sheriff, they call me Sombrero Jack. Why don't you respect a man's name?"

"Because I don't respect the man! What do you mean the Antrim kid should be in jail?"

"I mean he's the real criminal in this town, not me. I could tell you all about his stealing and killing, if you would listen."

Harvey walked closer to the cell. "Which Antrim kid are you talking about, Henry or Josie?"

"Henry, goddammit! Henry Antrim! The kid's a thief. He won't admit it, but everyone I know says that he's been stealing from people all year."

"That's nothing new to me, Harvey said. "I've been hearing the same story. I can't prove any of it or he'd be locked up. Tell me something new, or I'm going home."

"They say he's as mean a kid as you'll ever meet. I heard he once beheaded a kitten with his penknife. They say he did it just to satisfy his own cruelty."

"Never heard that one," Harvey said, laughing out loud and shaking his head in disbelief.

"He told me he killed a man, killed him for insulting his mother."

"What's the name of the man he killed?" Harvey asked.

"I don't know. I just know he's always bragging. Says he knifed a man for insulting his mother. Said he'd gut me if I said anything bad about her. He's proud of what he's done. He's a rotten seed, I'm telling you."

Harvey had never heard anyone say Henry was a killer, but figured it was a possibility. His own son had been on the wrong end of Henry's anger, and rumors had circulated for months that Henry had once tried to kill his own stepfather. The boy was certainly devoted to his mother and just might have killed someone for saying something unkind about her.

"Is it true that Henry beat you up in the Morrill Opera House?" Harvey asked.

"Truer than sunshine and moonlight. Kicked me in the ribs. Made it hard to sleep for weeks."

"I'd almost bet you had it coming," Harvey said.

Harvey had heard enough and left George alone to wash away his drunkenness. Harvey planned to go home and take a second look at the town's unsolved murders in the morning. Silver City had several killings that had been dismissed as crimes committed by migrant prospectors. Maybe one of those killings could be linked to Henry McCarty. Harvey knew better than to take George Schaefer's allegations too seriously. Even so, the murder issue was at least worth looking at. If Henry had killed someone, even some anonymous drunk insulting his mother, he would need to be put in jail.

— 52 —

Henry awoke the next morning to the sound of someone knocking on the door of his room at the boarding house. When he pushed the door open he saw Harvey Whitehill and Mrs. Brown standing in the hallway looking grim. Henry knew they weren't paying him a cordial visit.

"I need to talk with you," Harvey said, stepping into Henry's cramped quarters. Henry sat on his bed wearing the charcoal-colored long underwear that had become too tight to fit him comfortably. Mrs. Brown remained in the doorway.

"Last night I locked up a fella named George Schaefer," Harvey said, staring at Henry as if he was studying every reaction for signs of guilt. "Do you know him?"

"Yes," Henry said. "He stayed in the room next to this one for a few days."

"He moved out," Mrs. Brown said. "He told me he was leaving town."

"If so, he's come back," Harvey said. "I had him locked up last night and he's implicated Henry in a few crimes. Forgive me, Mrs. Brown, but I'd like to have a private talk with this boy."

Even though Mrs. Brown walked away, Henry sensed her reluctance to leave. She was the type who would love nothing more than having something more to gossip about.

"I told you I'd be watching you!" Harvey said, barking like a mad dog. "This Schaefer fellow tells me you killed a man."

"Killed a man? Was he drunk when he told you that?"

"I'm not here to talk about whether George Schaefer was drunk. I just want to know what you been up to."

"I'm telling you, Mr. Whitehill, I've never killed anyone."

"From what I know, you seem to have it in you to kill someone. You almost killed my son. I heard you pulled a knife on your stepfather."

"It's true that anger's got the best of me a few times," Henry said. "I'll admit that. But I've never killed anyone."

"I heard you killed a man for insulting your mother."

177

"Where'd you hear that?"

"Is it true?"

Henry hoped that at least the tone of his voice would convince Harvey he was telling the truth. "I'm being railroaded, Mr. Whitehill. I've never killed anyone. I've never stole anything. I've been trying to tell people for months that they been throwing false accusations at me."

"I'll admit that you've got no guilt in your manner," Harvey said. "But I'll need more than just hearing your side of the story. Seems like every time I turn around people are saying you're involved in something bad."

"I've heard that only the good looking girls like outlaws," Henry said, smiling. "That's the reason I'll always have ugly girlfriends, and those ugly girls should be all the proof you'll ever need to know that I'm no lawbreaker."

Harvey seemed to ignore Henry's attempt at lightening the mood.

"Why don't you talk with Miss Richards and the Truesdells?" Henry said. "They'll vouch for me."

"If you've done nothing wrong, you've got nothing to worry about."

"I'd hope not, but based on how quickly people accept the accusations against me, I'm starting to wonder."

"I stand by what I told you. If you've done nothing wrong, you have nothing to worry about." Harvey opened the door and walked into the hallway. "Keep your eyes on that boy," he said to Mrs. Brown as he left the boarding house.

Henry did not want to look at Mrs. Brown's suspicious scowl and shut the door to his room. Sitting on his bed with his head in his hands, he realized that he could not remain in Silver City. His reputation as a miscreant wasn't going away, and now he had Harvey Whitehill wondering whether he had killed a man. Silver City would be better off without him, he figured, and he would be better off living someplace where no one knew his reputation as a thief. It was time to leave Silver City and put the place that George Schaefer referred to as "this rathole" behind him.

Not until several hours later did Henry think about the bundle of items that George Schaefer had given him. The package was still under his bed, and he wished he had shown it to Harvey. In any case, forgetting about the package didn't matter much. He would soon be leaving Silver City forever.

— 53 —

Henry wasted an entire morning looking for Josie. He had wanted to tell his brother that he was leaving town, but Josie was nowhere to be found, and Henry could not continue to look much longer. The sooner he left town, the better. Josie would have to learn from someone else that his brother had left Silver City.

After giving up his search for Josie, Henry returned to the boarding house to gather his belongings. He would pay Mrs. Brown the dollar and a quarter he owed her and then leave town and head for Arizona Territory that afternoon.

As he walked into Mrs. Brown's parlor to pay his rent, he could see she was ready to confront him about something. Maybe she had decided to throw him out of the boarding house. If so, he would be telling her that he had wanted to leave anyway.

"Sheriff Whitehill told me to keep my eye on you, and I don't like what you've been doing," Mrs. Brown said.

"The way people greet me, I might as well start wearing a sign that lets everyone know I'm no thief."

"This is a serious situation, young man. I need to know why you have two guns in your room."

Henry felt as if someone had thrown a brick at him. He wished he had either thrown George's package away or given it to Harvey. Now it was too late.

"I appreciate you giving me a place to stay, Mrs. Brown, but all I want to do is pay you the money I owe you, gather my things, and leave."

"I don't think you're going anywhere. I was cleaning your room today and found a trunk under your bed. I looked in that trunk and couldn't believe you brought copies of *The Police Gazette* into my home. I don't approve of anyone reading that publication, especially in my home, and I certainly don't think a boy your age should be owning guns. I told the sheriff about what I found, and he's been looking for you."

At that moment Harvey Whitehill walked through the door of the boarding house.

Henry looked at Harvey and saw no sign of the good-natured man he had once known. Harvey looked like a man determined to save the good citizens of Silver City from a delinquent boy.

"I hear you have two guns," Harvey said. "Charlie Sun reported guns stolen from his laundry over a week ago, and I'd like to take a look at what you have in your room."

Henry had already thought that George had stolen the guns and clothes from Charlie Sun. He also thought that Harvey would never believe he had nothing to do with stealing them.

Harvey grabbed Henry's arm and escorted him down the hallway with Mrs. Brown following close behind. Henry knew his fate was sealed when Harvey asked him to pull his trunk from under the bed and pull the lid up.

"Two .44 percussion revolvers and an army blanket," Harvey said, unwrapping the bundle of items in Henry's trunk. "And what the hell are you doing with a pile of men's clothes too large to fit you. These clothes are for men twice your size."

Harvey looked into Henry's eyes like he was studying him for an answer. Henry looked away.

"Must be a hundred dollars worth of goods in this trunk," Harvey said. "All of it fitting the description of what Charlie Sun told me was missing."

Henry remained silent, wondering whether it was worth the effort to tell a story Harvey would not believe.

"I couldn't give a rat's rear end about you stealing from a Chinaman," Harvey told him, "but the blanket and clothes belonged to Charlie's customers, and you sure as hell don't need to be owning guns. It looks to me like you're in more trouble than you'll know how to handle."

"I didn't steal anything," Henry said. "I don't know what else I can say."

"Goddammit, Henry! If you didn't steal these things, tell me who did. Tell me why these things are in your room if you didn't steal them."

Harvey's anger frightened Henry, and he felt his eyes moisten.

"You've got to take care of yourself, young man. If you didn't take these things, you have to tell me who did or you're not leaving me any choice but to lock you up."

Harvey asked Henry to put his hands in front of him. After placing cuffs on Henry's hands, Harvey adjusted the ratchets.

Tears ran down Henry's cheeks, and he was embarrassed that Harvey was seeing him cry.

"They're too tight," Henry said, struggling to free his hands.

"I hate to consider what your mother would think of this."

Harvey pushed Henry out the door and escorted him down Yankie Street toward the jailhouse where he was locked in a cell. Once Henry was in the cell, Harvey unlocked the cuffs, and for that, Henry was grateful. He was not grateful to be left alone that evening with no candle or lantern to light the cell.

Sitting in the dark, Henry thought about the mistake he had made accepting the bundle of stolen items from George Schaefer. George was a thief, someone who could not be trusted, and it didn't take a clever mind to figure that out. Henry should have known better than to accept anything George gave him. He should never have believed a word George said.

Henry also thought about all the false accusations against him. People had been quick to blame him for crimes he didn't commit, and now he was sitting in a jail cell. He was determined to find a way out, and when he did, he would leave Silver City. He would go far away and live someplace where his reputation would not follow him.

— 54 —

Early the next morning Harvey dragged a lead pipe across the bars of Henry's cell.

"It's too late in the day to still be in bed," Harvey told Henry, his voice booming through the jailhouse.

Henry had not been asleep, but the racket created by the lead pipe caused him to bolt up from his prone position on the cot. He had been awake all night — a rainstorm making his cell too cold to fall asleep.

When he saw Charlie Sun standing next to Harvey he knew what trouble awaited him. Charlie had already told Harvey that the items in Henry's trunk had been taken from the laundry. Charlie claimed that three other blankets were missing, as well as two sets of clothes. Henry only had one blanket and one set of clothes in the trunk, and when Charlie described the missing items, Harvey looked up with a smug grin on his face. Henry could tell that Harvey thought he had just solved the crime.

"The Schaefer boy was wearing those clothes the night I arrested him," Harvey said, looking at Henry. "I'd bet that you and George worked together to steal from this Chinaman. I'd also bet that George was the kingfish. You're too young and rawboned to lead someone like George into a criminal act. Did George give you that bundle of goods?"

"Yes," Henry said, surprised that Harvey had finally asked the right question.

"Did he steal them from the Chinaman?"

"I'm assuming," Henry said. "He had told me he wanted to steal from Mr. Sun, and asked me to go along. I wouldn't agree to it. I wanted no part of his schemes. He told me he was moving out of the boarding house and gave me a package to hold for him until he returned. I put it in my trunk and when he didn't return, I decided I'd bring it to you, but I forgot about it."

"No need to tell tales," Harvey said. "Stick with the truth and you won't have to change your story later."

"That is the truth."

"When did George give those things to you?"

"A week ago Wednesday."

"Did he give you more blankets than I found in your room?"

"No."

"Did he give you a new pair of brown trousers?"

"No."

"Did he give you a blue shirt with white squares decorating it?"

"No, sir," Henry said. "Have you asked George these questions?"

"As far as I can tell, that catamite's left town forever. People are going to be happy to see that at least I got you locked up."

Henry's eyes danced around the room as he looked for a way out of his cell.

"What do you have to say for yourself?" Harvey asked.

"I've already told you I didn't steal anything."

"You're in a warehouse of trouble," Harvey said. He almost sounded like he felt sorry for Henry. "A little discipline from your mother might have prevented you from becoming a thief. Maybe all you need is a little time in jail to turn you in the right direction."

"I'll say it again, I didn't steal anything." Henry didn't know what else to say.

"The crime against the Chinaman is more than petty theft," Harvey said. "The clothes don't matter a goddamn, but the value of those two guns could put you in territorial prison for seven years."

Charlie Sun, still standing next to Harvey, nodded his approval.

"George stole from the Chinaman," Henry said. "I'm no thief."

"The stolen items in your trunk are damning evidence," Harvey said. "Looks to me like we've finally got some proof that we can use to lock you up."

"The boy's a thief," Charlie Sun said, looking into Henry's nervous eyes.

"I'll let you sit in this cell for a time and think about what you've done," Harvey said. "Think about what your mama would have thought of you."

"Leave my Mam out of this." Henry snapped.

"I'm going to keep you here for now," Harvey said. "It's the best jail in the area, just uncomfortable enough to teach you a lesson. I'll bring Justice Givens in here tomorrow. He'll tell me what to do with you."

Henry said nothing, his eyes darting around the cell. The dark, confined quarters made him claustrophobic, and the smell of urine and feces made him want to vomit.

"I imagine Justice Givens will send you before a grand jury, which will only be the beginning of your troubles. Looks like we may be keeping you here a couple of months before they end up sending you to prison."

— 55 —

Isaac Givens arrived at the jailhouse early the next morning, his back ramrod straight and his face frozen in an unforgiving frown. When Henry looked at Justice Givens he saw a man with no empathy, a man hardened by the ways of the world.

"What's the boy done wrong?" Isaac asked Harvey, drawing on his tightly rolled tobacco.

Harvey answered in a matter-of-fact tone, sounding as if he didn't even know Henry. "Almost two weeks ago the Chinaman

185

Charlie Sun reported army blankets and clothing stolen from his laundry. The thief also took two .44 percussion revolvers, making the value of stolen items enough to send someone to territorial prison."

"What's it got to do with this boy?"

"This boy, named Henry McCarty, rented a room at Mrs. Brown's boarding house. Mrs. Brown found one of the blankets, some of the clothing, and both guns in a trunk under the boy's bed. The situation implicates the boy in the theft."

Henry would have rolled his eyes at Harvey's note of formality, but knew enough not to antagonize anyone deciding his fate.

"Sounds like a clear case of larceny," Givens said, sucking in more tobacco smoke. "Keep him here until the next session of the grand jury. After that, we'll have a trial. It looks like we may have to send him to prison."

Justice Givens then left the jailhouse, giving Henry no opportunity to speak for himself and tell the truth about what had happened.

"It's best that you spend some time sitting on that cot thinking about how to set yourself right," Harvey told Henry. "You've been chasing the wrong values since your mama died, and it's now time to do some thinking about what you've done. Not much else to do in a jail cell, I suppose."

Harvey went home soon after Justice Givens walked out, leaving Henry alone in his cell, guarded only by the town's deputy, a fussy man named Dan Tucker.

— 56 —

Harry Whitehill was prepared to confront his father about what had happened to Henry. Word had spread through town that his father wanted to put Henry in prison, and when Harry told his mother and sister Emma about Henry's situation, they were also outraged by the news.

Harry liked Henry, even though Henry had once assaulted him. Harry understood the reason Henry had attacked him and was willing to forgive him.

Harry's mother and sister also liked Henry. Neither of them thought Henry was a thief, and they had said they would stand shoulder to shoulder with Harry, ready to defend the boy when Harvey came home that evening.

"Henry didn't steal from the Chinaman," Harry said, greeting his father at the door, not even giving him time to take off his coat. "You shouldn't be sending him to jail!"

"Surely you know what everyone else knows about Sombrero Jack," Emma said to her father, her voice trembling with emotion. "You need to go back and unlock Henry from that cell. He's done nothing wrong."

"Everyone knows that George Schaefer is a troublemaker," Harry said. "He's the one who stole from the Chinaman, not Henry. Everyone knows that Henry's being punished unfairly."

"That boy has deserved some form of punishment for a long time," Harvey said, finally taking off his coat and hanging it by the door. "I've talked to Henry enough to sense he's headed in the wrong direction unless I do something to set him straight."

Harry had known for months that he could have ended the

accusations that were ruining Henry's reputation. A confession that he and his cousin Charley had stolen from Matt Derbyshire would have cleared Henry's name and explained why Henry had attacked him in front of Bailey's Drug Store. But Harry had no desire to get Charley or himself in trouble, and he feared his father's wrath. He had no idea why Henry had not already told everyone what had happened, but was grateful for Henry's silence and relieved that circumstances had given him an opportunity to make amends with Henry. Harry wanted to clear his conscience by persuading his father to let Henry go.

"You've got to let Henry out of that cell," Harry pleaded. "He's not the thief you think he is."

Emma, with her jaw set firm, stood directly in front of her father. "You've made a mistake locking Henry up. He's done nothing wrong. You told us when his mother was alive that she had raised two good boys. You were right. He *is* a good boy, and he's certainly no thief."

Harry had never heard Emma speak to her father in such a tone.

"Talk to Miss Richards," Emma continued. "She'll tell you that Henry is well-behaved. If you could talk to Sarah Abraham, she would tell you that Henry is a gentleman."

"You should listen to your children," Harry's mother said, joining the chorus of protest. "Harry and Emma are telling the truth. You didn't take the job as sheriff to punish innocent boys, did you?"

"Henry might be innocent of *this* crime," Harvey said. "George Schaefer causes trouble everywhere he goes, and if I could get him back in jail, I'm certain I could get him to admit he's the one who stole from the Chinaman."

"Why is Henry in jail then?" Harry asked.

" Because he's been in trouble ever since his mama died."

"That's not true," Emma said.

"That is true," Harvey said. "Long before I became sheriff I had heard about Henry's crimes, and I've heard —"

"The accusations were never true," Emma said, cutting her father short. "The people of this town are wrong about Henry McCarty. They don't know him like we do. Sarah was my best friend and she told me all about him. He's the victim of a reputation he doesn't deserve."

"Listen to me," Harvey said. "Henry's been involved in several crimes over the last year. Just look at what he did to Harry outside that drug store. Almost drowned him."

Harry thought about telling the truth and explaining the reason Henry had attacked him, but chose to remain silent. He was terrified of what his father might do if he knew the whole story, and he was grateful that Emma didn't know that he and Charley had stolen from Mr. Derbyshire. If she had known, she would not have been able to keep it to herself and would have told their father.

"I shouldn't be telling you this," Harvey said, "but I had a talk with Justice Givens this afternoon. I spoke to him about how Henry's just a boy and maybe we shouldn't put him in front of a grand jury."

"Does that mean you won't send him to prison?" Harry asked.

"That's right. But I'd prefer we kept that news to ourselves. It's better to let that boy sit in a jail cell for a few days and give him the scare he needs to place him on the right side of the law."

"That's not right," Harry's mother said. "All you'll do is scare

189

that boy into leaving town when he gets out. He's done nothing wrong, and he shouldn't be spending any time in a jail cell."

"You've got to trust me and let me do the right thing," Harvey said. "All I'm doing is trying to give that boy the parenting he's needed since his mama passed away."

"His mother would have never wanted him in a jail cell," Harry's mother said.

"Trust me," Harvey said. "Someday he'll be a better man for what I'm doing."

For Harry, who had not wanted his father knowing the entire story, the situation could not have turned out better. If Henry had been put on trial with the possibility of going to territorial prison, Harry's conscience would have forced him into making a confession. Letting Henry sit for only a few days in a jail cell was a much better alternative. Harry just hoped Henry would not betray him and tell his father about what he and Charley had done.

— 57 —

Henry received food three times a day from Dan Tucker. Twice a day, Dan gave him a broom.

"Sweep that cell and slide your pisspot through the door," Dan told him. "I like to keep this place clean."

"This place can't be cleaned up," Henry said. "It's been soiled until the end of time. I could clean a privy outside a rancher's bunkhouse easier than this place."

"Smart comments won't bring you any sympathy from me or Harvey," Dan said. "Do as your told and get that cell swept clean."

Other than Dan Tucker, with his lanky frame, dark eyes, and

wilted mustache, Henry had not seen another person since the previous day when Harvey paid a visit with Justice Givens.

When Harvey finally returned that morning, Henry wished he had stayed away. Harvey's visit amounted to no more than another tongue lashing and a pile of threats.

"The grand jury will indict you," Harvey said. "They'll put you in front of a judge and jury and then you'll go to prison. Figure on seven years."

Henry sat quietly on his cot with his knees pulled to his chest, not knowing what to say. The idea of going to prison scared him, and his eyes danced from one part of the room to another looking for a way to escape. The only way he could see out of the jailhouse — other than though the big oak door leading to the sheriff's office — was a small vent on the wall above him.

"I'm seeing the criminal nature in your eyes," Harvey said. If you're not taught a lesson now, you'll be nothing but trouble down the road. Whether you're living in Silver City or somewhere else, you'll be someone who's always living on the wrong side of the law."

Henry thought Harvey could not have been more wrong if he had been predicting snow in July. He was no criminal. He was simply terrified about going to prison. Couldn't Harvey see that?

"Are you ready to admit that you helped George Schaefer steal from the Chinaman?" Harvey asked.

Henry remained quiet.

Harvey looked at him for a long minute without saying anything, waiting for him to answer.

"You can get yourself out of trouble by merely telling the truth," Harvey continued. "Judges aren't as harsh on those who admit their crimes."

"I see no reason to admit to something I didn't do."

Henry's arms cradled his chest. Without a blanket there was no way to stay warm. A draft came through the opening ten feet above him, an opening blocked by bars covering a hole no larger than half a loaf of bread. It was too small to crawl through, but big enough to make sure the air in the jail cell matched the temperature outdoors.

"You look cold," Harvey said.

"I am," Henry said. "It was freezing in here last night, and I can't get warm."

"I'll get my wife to send you some socks and blankets. I'll also get some wood for that fireplace down the hall. Looks like the cold weather has come early this year."

"This cell's too small, it's musty, it's soiled, and it smells like an outhouse," Henry said. "It's making me sick."

"I'd say that's fair punishment for all you've done," Harvey said.

"Couldn't you unlock my cell and let me walk around the corridor to warm myself up a little? I'm the only one you've got in jail right now, and you can keep that oak door to the corridor locked. No one would ever be able to break that thing down."

Henry hoped his request sounded reasonable. A single hallway branched away from the sheriff's office with jail cells on either side. A heavy door separated the office from the hallway, a door that Harvey could lock, leaving Henry free to roam around and get a little exercise.

"I guess we could do that," Harvey said. "It shouldn't do no harm as long as I lock you in the corridor and leave Dan in the other room watching the door."

"Thank you," Henry said.

"I'm going home to get some socks and more blankets for you.

I'll need to lock you back in your cell when I return. We've got too much to do around here to let you walk that hallway all day."

"Give Mrs. Whitehill my best, and tell her I appreciate whatever she can send," Henry said, trying to show Harvey the good manners his mother had taught him.

— 58 —

After Harvey locked the door, Henry walked into the hallway. Trying to remain quiet, he placed his tattered moccasins with their stiff rawhide soles in the corner of his cell and then walked down the hallway in his bare feet. At the end of the corridor stood a fireplace. He looked up the chimney and saw a thick layer of soot coating its stone walls.

He shoved his head into the flue and forced his shoulders up the chimney to find out whether his body was small enough to fit. Pulling himself back out, he thought for a moment about the task in front of him and figured he could do it. He might face the embarrassment of getting stuck, requiring Harvey or Dan to pull him out, but he had to take the chance. For once, he hoped, his undersized body was about to get him out of trouble, rather than bring trouble his way.

Not wanting to make himself any wider than necessary, he removed his belt. He then squatted in front of the fireplace and shoved both arms up the chimney, clasping his hands above his head. He pushed himself up with his legs and then used his elbows to pull himself into the tiny passage that would begin his twelve-foot journey to freedom. Sharp rocks cut his arms and legs as he inched his way high enough that he could finally use his feet to catch stones jutting from the fireplace and thrust himself upward. With his entire body crammed into a space too small for most dogs, he had to close his mouth to keep from breathing soot into his lungs. About the time the anxiety from being in such a confined space made him regret what he had begun, he arrived at the top of the chimney and bright sunlight washed over his blackened face.

With his hands free, he pulled himself onto the top of the chimney before stepping gently onto the flat roof. He wanted to make sure that Dan Tucker would not hear his footsteps. He then hurried across the roof to the back of the jailhouse, moving away from Hudson Street so that a passerby would not spot him and spoil his escape.

At the back wall of the jailhouse he looked at the ground ten feet below him. Even though he might break a leg, he figured he had no choice other than jumping off the side. At least he was on the opposite side of the building from the sheriff's office, and Dan would probably not hear him fall. He jumped feet first and hit the ground with a thud, causing him to tumble forward face first into the dirt. As far as he could tell, nothing was broken.

Lying on the ground with his clothes torn and bloodied, covered in soot, he got up and ran east, a direction that took him even farther away from Hudson Street. Looking for somewhere to hide, he spotted a storage shack at the foot of the hill behind the jailhouse. Inside, he found a hatchet that he used to pull up a floorboard. He then rolled under the floor and set the board back in place. Scores of cockroaches scurried across his body, making him as uneasy as a wet cat, but he had nowhere else to go and decided to persevere until nightfall. He couldn't be seen on the streets of Silver City in daylight without taking the chance that someone would report him to Harvey and have him thrown back into jail.

As far as he knew, no one had seen him come out the chimney. If so, they would have seen him from Hudson Street and would have had no idea where he went after jumping from the roof. If no one found him in the shed, he'd be safe until after the sun went down and he could leave the shack to find somewhere else to hide.

— 59 —

Less than an hour after Harvey had left the jailhouse he returned with socks and blankets for Henry. After he unlocked the door to the corridor he was surprised to find Henry's cell empty.

"Goddammit, Dan! Where's the boy? You're supposed to be watching him."

Harvey looked to the far end of the hallway, saw a belt lying in front of the fireplace and knew immediately what had happened. He ran toward the fireplace, hoping to catch Henry stuck inside. Seeing daylight as he looked up, he wondered how anyone, even a boy as small as Henry, could crawl up that chimney. The damned thing seemed too small to contain his own right arm. But he could see no other way out. Thinking he needed to stretch some barbed wire over both ends of the chimney, he knew that first he needed to find Henry McCarty.

"You had no more to do than watch that boy and make sure he didn't cause mischief." Harvey said to Dan. "I can't believe you didn't at least hear him walking across the roof."

Harvey and Dan ran outside and looked at the hills east of Silver City. An old Mexican wearing a red and black sombrero sat on a rock behind the jailhouse and asked Harvey if he was looking for the boy who had come out the chimney.

"Yes," Harvey said. "Did you see which way he went?"

The old man pointed toward Hudson Street and told Harvey that Henry had run up the street going north.

"He couldn't have gone far," Dan said. "He's probably running toward Central City." Harvey and Dan then ran up Hudson Street, away from the jailhouse.

Harvey spent the remainder of the day searching for Henry. He went to Mrs. Brown's to see if Henry had collected his belongings. He went to the Exchange and to the Truesdells' home. He even visited the Abrahams' home. He ended the day having no idea where Henry went, feeling embarrassed that he had let a fifteen-year-old boy outwit him. If Henry had only stuck it out another few days, Harvey thought, he would have gone free without having to break the law by escaping.

— 60 —

Henry remained under the floor of the storage shack until long after sundown. Although he was hungry and had become so thirsty he had developed a cotton mouth, he stayed rooted to his spot in the dirt with the cockroaches. Not until late in the evening when the festive sounds from Main Street's saloons had begun to die down did he decide to leave the shack and find another place to hide.

After leaving the shack he sat on the hill behind the jailhouse and thought about where he would go next. He thought about heading out of town before the sun came up but had no moccasins for his feet and no horse to ride. He considered going to Miss Richards and asking for help, but figured it was too late to wake her.

His best option, he decided, was to go to the Truesdells' home. They would never mind him coming to them for help — even if it was late at night and even if he had just escaped from jail.

Staying in the shadows as he walked through town, he hoped the soot covering his body would hide him from anyone still wandering the streets. After arriving at the Truesdells' home, he tapped several times on a window at the back of the house, hoping to get someone to open the door and let him in. Finally, Chauncey came to the window.

"Henry!" Chauncey said, sounding surprised to see him. "Sheriff Whitehill was here this evening looking for you. How'd you get so dirty?"

"I pulled myself up a chimney, and I've been hiding under a woodshed."

"Come in before someone sees you."

Chauncey opened the back door and no sooner had Henry entered the house than Clara came into the parlor, greeting him with a hug in spite of the soot, blood, and dirt covering his body. Chauncey's father wasn't living in the house anymore, having moved away from his family several weeks earlier.

"Harvey said you had left town," Clara said.

"Not yet. Can I stay here?" Henry asked.

"Of course you can stay here."

It was the first time in days that Henry had sensed someone was on his side.

"I know you didn't steal from the Chinaman," Clara said. "I'm sure even Harvey knows that."

"Then why did he put me in jail?" Henry asked.

"He was just trying to scare you. I gave him an earful when he visited me. He said that even his own children and his wife had scolded him for arresting you."

"It doesn't appear their scolding did me any good."

"Makes no difference now. You need to get out of those clothes and clean yourself up."

Clara left the room for a moment and returned with an extra set of Chauncey's bedclothes.

"These may be too large for you, but it's all we have," she said. Clara handed Henry a basin full of water and a towel to clean himself. She then took his shirt and pants to scrub them on a washboard. "I can give you an old pair of Gerald's boots tomorrow. We'll stuff them with old rags and hope they fit you."

After much scrubbing, both Henry and his clothes were clean. Clara had hung his clothes by the wood stove to dry. Only then did she tell Henry and her own boys — Chauncey and Gideon — that they needed to get some sleep.

"We can't stay up all night," she said. "I'll see you in the morning, and we'll discuss what to do next after the sun comes up."

"No discussion is necessary," Henry said. "I've already decided what I'm going to do. I'm leaving town as soon as I can."

"Let's talk about it in the morning," Clara said, sounding like she wanted to have the last word before Henry and her boys went to bed.

Henry knew that nothing would change his determination to get away from Silver City.

— **61** —

The next morning Clara gave Henry a breakfast of hardtack

crackers and sliced peaches.

"I think you should return to Sheriff Whitehill," she told him as he sat down to eat.

Henry sensed her explanation would not be something he wanted to hear.

"If you go back, I'm sure Harvey will let you out of jail in a few days. I don't think he has any plans to send you to prison. The worst part will be the lecture he'll give you about running away."

"I've heard all the lectures I want," Henry said. "Mr. Whitehill's got his mind set on keeping me locked up. Even if he doesn't believe I stole from the Chinaman, he figures I'm guilty of other crimes. He's got no misgivings about making me pay a price."

"I don't believe that," Clara said. "I think he just wants to scare you."

"I wish I could believe you, but I think I need to get out of this town."

"Where will you go?"

"Mrs. Brown told me that my stepfather is living in Clifton. He owes me money. Maybe he'll at least give me a place to sleep."

"Why don't you first spend some time here with us and give me a chance to talk with Harvey? I'm sure I can talk some sense into him."

"If I stay here Mr. Whitehill will find me and put me back in jail. Even if he doesn't keep me in jail, the next time something is stolen I'll get blamed, and Mr. Whitehill will want to arrest me again. There's no talking sense to him. He's determined to get me in a jail cell and keep me there."

"I could send you to Ed Moulton's place on Bear Mountain. I'm certain he would let you hide there long enough for me to work on changing Harvey's mind."

"No ma'am. I appreciate you trying to help me, but I need to leave this town. I'll go and see my stepfather. He's got my Mam's money and owes me my share. Should be enough to keep me going for a time."

"I wish I could persuade you to stay."

"My mind's made up. I've never been more certain of anything."

Clara sighed and walked across the room to a freestanding cupboard. Inside, she found a small box, opened it, and removed a gold coin.

"This quarter eagle should get you to Clifton," she said. "I only knew your mother for a year, but she was the best friend I've had, and I see her whenever I look at you. I wish I could keep you here, but if I can't, I guess giving you some money is the least I can do for her."

Henry would miss Clara. No one had helped him more after his mother died.

"Thank you for the help," he said. "You can trust me that I will repay you."

"I wouldn't depend too much on your stepfather helping you," Clara said. "I want you to know that if things don't work out, you're always welcome back here. I'm still going to talk with Harvey. He'll understand the error of his ways once I've talked to him. When you come back, everything will be settled in your favor."

Henry figured Clara would never be able to change Harvey's mind. Besides, Henry planned on never returning to Silver City. It was time for him to leave and live somewhere else. It was time to begin a new life.

After eating more crackers and peaches, Henry said his

goodbyes.

"You've been a good friend," he said to Chauncey. "I hope I'm forgiven for smoking you out of that outhouse."

"All is forgiven," Chauncey said, laughing and shaking Henry's hand.

"I'm still mad at you," Clara said with a smile.

"Thank you for everything," Henry said, giving Clara a hug.

"It's time for the stage to come by," Clara said, her voice tightening. "Get out of here and enjoy your journey."

Henry left the Truesdells that morning and caught the stagecoach out of Silver City, leaving town before Harvey Whitehill or anyone else knew he was gone.

He was unsure of where he would end up living or what he would end up doing. He only knew that wherever he went he would make sure that people would say Catherine McCarty had raised a good man.

Arizona Territory
October 1875

— 62 —

Henry spent his first two weeks in Clifton running errands for saloonkeepers in exchange for meals. At night he slept next to the stagecoach terminus in an abandoned canvas tent. He had not yet found a way to make more money after spending what Clara had given him to pay for the stagecoach ride and a few meals.

He had asked several people in Clifton if they knew Bill Antrim but learned that most were reluctant to talk to a vagabond kid. One day, while cleaning tables in a saloon, his luck changed, and he met a man who volunteered the information he needed.

"I know Bill Antrim, and I know where he's living."

The man offering the information was sitting alone, tending to a glass of whiskey.

"Antrim's moved into a cabin next to the river. You'll find it just past the last cantina as you leave town."

"Bill Antrim's my stepfather," Henry said, taking a seat across from the man. "I was supposed to meet him here in Clifton but I haven't been able to find him."

"Time to quit looking. I just told you where he is."

"My name's Henry. Can I ask yours?"

"Nope. I figure Antrim's got no need to know who sent a piddling kid his way. He may be your stepfather, but he's a no good son-of-a-bitch. I'm hoping you bring him nothing but grief. From the looks of you, it appears that's exactly what you'll do."

"I'm assuming you don't like Bill Antrim," Henry said, laughing. "You and me should set up an organization for those who don't like that snake."

The man smiled. "You're certainly more of a charmer than he is. He cheated a friend of mine when we were working the Metcalf mines with him last year. He took a loan and hasn't paid it back. My friend gave up trying to get the money back, and if he'd been a different type of man your stepfather might not be alive today."

"He's cheated me, too," Henry said. "If you're right about where I can find him, maybe I can at least settle the score for myself."

"I wish you luck," the man said, "but I doubt that son-of-a-bitch would ever make good on what he owes other people. He lives for himself only."

"You've probably got him pegged right," Henry said, "but I've come a long way and need to at least try to take what he owes me. I figure that a man like him should at least be pestered a little."

The man smiled at Henry and again wished him luck.

— 63 —

Henry walked past the last cantina on the northern edge of town and just as he'd been told, he spotted a small cabin sitting next to the river.

As he approached the cabin he sensed that no one was around.

He then tapped on the door, calling to see if anyone was inside. When no one answered, he opened the door and stepped inside.

The cabin was smaller than the one where Henry had lived with his family in Silver City. Against the north wall Henry saw a shovel, a couple of mining pans, and a pickaxe. A stove sat in the southeast corner, although Henry couldn't see any cooking utensils. With no cot inside, Henry assumed the person living in the cabin must have been placing a bedroll next to the west wall. It was the only area of the cabin that provided an open space on the floor. A small table with a single chair had been placed opposite the cleared-out space.

Henry saw few personal belongings. Nothing looked familiar, and he wondered whether he was standing in Bill's home. If so, Bill had taken several steps backward from his life in Wichita, where he had once owned a home with four rooms and more than his share of household goods.

Only when Henry saw a picture of his mother did he knew for certain that the cabin belonged to Bill Antrim. The tintype sat on top of a crate next to the door. While living in Wichita Henry's mother had once asked a photographer to take her picture as payment for laundry. As far as Henry knew, there was only one copy of the photograph. He had not seen it since leaving Kansas and had not known that Bill had it.

Henry picked the tintype up and was overwhelmed by a desire to hear his mother's Irish brogue. He put the picture in his pocket, figuring there was no need for Bill to keep it.

"What the hell are you doing here?"

Henry looked up and saw Bill standing in the doorway. He looked ten years older — his face well worn and his eyes tired. Henry assumed Bill hadn't seen him put the tintype in his pocket. If so, he certainly would have said something.

"I've been trying to find you," Henry said.

"I won't say it's good to see you. I wish you hadn't come."

After an awkward moment when Henry didn't know what to say, Bill broke the silence. "Would you like to eat?" he asked, sounding like he hoped Henry would refuse the offer and leave.

"I certainly could eat," Henry said. "I haven't had a meal since yesterday."

"I don't think you can call what I'm getting ready to share with you a meal. I don't have much to my name these days. All I've got is a little flour and salt sitting in the bags hanging from my burro. I might also have a little dried beef."

Henry followed Bill outside to the burro that had been tied to the side of the cabin. The animal was too small to ride but large enough to pack Bill's meager possessions. Henry untied the cooking utensils hanging from the animal while Bill reached inside a pack bag and pulled out a few strips of jerky.

"Get some rainwater from the barrel and we'll make hardtack," Bill said. "We'll top it off with this beef."

"That sounds good," Henry said. "I'm starving."

After Henry started a fire, Bill made a few biscuits. Bill and Henry then sat down to eat. Bill sat in a chair next to the table while Henry sat on the floor, resting his back against the closed door.

"Why'd you come to Clifton?" Bill asked.

"I thought I'd see if I could join you in prospecting. I'm a hard worker."

"I don't need any help. You're better off looking for work somewhere else."

"I'm already helping two different saloonkeepers. They feed me now and then, but I need a place to live. I could ask them for wages instead of food and then pay you my share to live here."

Bill did not respond to the offer. "I suppose it's been tough since your mama died," he said

"You taking Mam's money didn't help."

"That money don't concern you."

"I figure that money's as much mine and Josie's as yours. Mam would have wanted her own flesh and blood to have it, and I came to get my share."

"The money's gone. Gambled away. I'll never see it again."

From the few possessions Henry could see in the cabin, Bill must have been telling the truth. It didn't look like Bill had much, if any, money.

"I've got nothing to give you," Bill said, "even if I wanted to help you. Look around and you'll see the total of my belongings."

"Looks like you've squandered away everything you carried from Kansas."

"What I did with my possessions is none of your business."

"That may be so," Henry said, "but what you did with Mam's money is certainly my business."

Bill didn't respond.

Henry, deciding he couldn't stand to look at the son-of-a-bitch any longer, stood up and gathered the pots and dishes for cleaning. He then walked to the river to wash them, while Bill remained in the cabin rolling tobacco.

After returning to the cabin, Henry pleaded with Bill, "I need a place to stay. Couldn't I at least stay here until I find my own place? The fall weather's making it too cold to sleep outside. I'll work for my share."

"This cabin's not made for two."

"I have nowhere else to go."

Henry hated to beg the son-of-a-bitch, but couldn't stand the thought of sleeping another night on the cold ground with no blanket. At least Bill had a stove and a pile of wood to keep him warm.

"Why don't you go back to Silver City?" Bill said. "There's nothing for you here."

"I can't go back. Harvey Whitehill's the sheriff now and he wants me in jail."

"Why would Harvey want you in jail?"

"He thinks I stole some laundry and a couple of guns from a Chinaman, but I didn't steal anything."

"Why would Harvey think you stole something if you didn't?"

"A fellow named George Schaefer stole those things and asked me to keep them for him."

"I knew that fella when I worked in Georgetown. He called himself Sombrero Jack." Bill spoke as if he was thinking about an old friend. "He was a fun fella, but I can see how he might get you in trouble."

"Harvey thought George dragged me into stealing," Henry explained, "but I'm telling you I had nothing to do with it."

"The way I see it," Bill said, inhaling his tobacco, "if you'd done nothing wrong, Harvey wouldn't want you in a jail cell."

Henry shrugged. He had grown accustomed to others not believing what he said.

Bill leaned forward in his chair and looked Henry in the eye. "Get back to Silver City and straighten things out with Harvey," he said. "There's nothing I can do for you."

"It's no use going back. Mr. Whitehill is determined to lock me up, and nothing I say makes a difference. I've been branded a thief in that town."

Bill leaned back in his chair. "I'm more inclined to believe Harvey, especially if he's the sheriff. I'm assuming you probably are a thief, and if that's the type of boy you are, you shouldn't be in my home. Sounds to me like your reputation alone would bring trouble my way."

Henry wondered why he had ever come to Clifton. He wondered why he had ever expected he might get help from his stepfather. "I hope you had fun pissing Mam's money away," he said.

"The money's gone, and I want you gone," Bill said. "No need to drag me into your problems. I've got too many other things to worry about."

Henry had nothing left to say, and after a few seconds of silence he left the cabin. He did not bother to say goodbye as he walked out. He never wanted to see Bill Antrim again.

Outside, unseen by Bill, Henry searched through the pack bags hanging on the burro. He grabbed the last of the beef jerky from one bag and a handgun from the other. Putting the gun and jerky in his pocket next to the picture of his mother, he decided to take the items as his own.

"Might as well be the thief they say I am," he whispered to himself as he walked away from his stepfather's cabin.

— 64 —

Henry returned to Clifton, working for scraps of food from saloonkeepers. He continued to sleep in the tent next to the stagecoach terminus, although he would need someplace warmer before the freezing storms of late fall hit town. Until then, he would make do with a piece of canvas to keep him out of the rain.

One afternoon, while emptying a bucket of water into a pig trough, he spotted Bill coming toward him from about fifty yards down the street. Not wanting to explain why he had stolen items from Bill's pack bags, he hid behind a cistern at the side of a mercantile store. He then stood motionless until Bill passed him on the way toward a saloon next to the store.

As he waited, he realized he would never be able to avoid Bill as long as he remained in Clifton. It was time to leave, and he had an idea where he would go next. He had heard miners and ranchers at the Exchange talking about a new mining camp in Arizona Territory called Globe City. It was located over a hundred miles from Clifton, and Henry figured it would be as good a place as any to find work. Besides, he had nowhere else to go, and if he wanted to stay away from Bill, he needed to get out of Clifton.

Early the next morning he left for Globe City, walking toward the Gila River with no possessions other than the picture of his mother and the gun he had taken from Bill. He had already eaten the jerky he had stolen from Bill, and he left town with no other food. He had no loads for his gun and no burro to ride. He had no money to pay for a stagecoach, and he certainly couldn't afford a meal at the cantina as he left town.

He had not looked in a mirror in several weeks and could only imagine how he would look to others when he arrived in Globe City. He had always been nothing more than a small-framed, rat-faced kid, and he knew it. He had not bathed since long before Harvey Whitehill put him in jail, and his body reeked with the rank smell of every place he had been since leaving Silver City. His shirt and pants were too small and full of holes, and he was wearing Gerald Truesdell's man-sized boots stuffed with old rags. His hair had grown below his ears in uncombed curls that were encrusted with mud.

He understood that the food and other possessions he needed would never come his way until he found employment, but he wondered if he would ever be able to find a job. He wondered whether anyone would want to hire an undersized boy to do the man's work of ranching or mining. He wasn't even sure he would find work in a saloon. After all, why would an establishment of any kind want to put a scruffy vagrant like him in front of its patrons? Even the unwashed prospectors, gamblers, and whores of a dusty mining camp would probably find him too unkempt for serving food and drinks. All he could do was get to Globe City and see if he might find someone willing to hire him. He was willing to do anything for money — anything that paid him enough to buy a meal.

Five days into his journey he began to pay a price for trying to walk across the desert unprepared. Mr. Truesdell's boots were too large, and the rags stuffed inside had not kept his feet from slipping out. He had thrown the boots away and had been walking barefoot for two days. His feet were now rubbed raw and bleeding, sending streaks of scarlet flowing down the Gila River whenever he stepped into the water. He suffered from a throbbing pain that began in his toes and spread throughout his legs. Only the agony of his empty stomach competed with the pain radiating from his feet. He had eaten nothing other than a few fig beetles since leaving Clifton.

He had heard that he should head north from the Gila after

passing the San Carlos, but he was beginning to wonder if he would ever reach the San Carlos. He had been walking five days and had seen no signs of the tributary that marked the point where he should head north. As he watched the sunset's bright rays of red and orange flare from behind the mountains on the horizon, he only hoped that tomorrow would be the day that would bring him to the San Carlos.

He also hoped he might finally get a good night's sleep. Sleeping on the rocky riverbed of the Gila was not easy, especially with his fear of the night, a fear he had never known before. Since he had left Clifton, nighttime seemed to distort the good sense his mother had given him, and he had begun to dread the sun going down. It was late October, but it felt like mid-December, and darkness forced him to confront the frigid night air of the desert without a blanket to protect him. Rain had fallen every evening after he left Clifton. He could not stay dry and could not keep a fire burning long enough to get warm. He spent his nights frightened by the snakes and other creatures that might get at him while he tried to sleep.

He was also disturbed by the ramblings of his own mind that kept him awake, the torturous thoughts and visions ignited by darkness. He was plagued by images of his mother's corpse, her lifeless eyes staring at him from her grave. He was tormented by his memory of the New York riot he had witnessed as a child, an event he had told his mother he didn't remember. He had lied. He could still see the mob lynching that colored man, pushing that poor soul to his death from a balcony. He could still hear the screams of the man's wife and daughter piercing the night air as they were beaten to death.

"Justice," one of the murderers had said to him at the time.

"Justice."

His mother had told him there was a wickedness within everyone, a wickedness ready to unleash itself if it was not kept locked up. He had learned that his mother was right. He had seen the wickedness in others, those who had wronged him and taken away his chance for a good life in Silver City.

Now, on the banks of the Gila River, doing his best to make it through the night, he was beginning to see the wickedness within himself, within the ideas and images in his mind over which he had no control. He thought about the satisfaction that would come his way if he could take revenge against George Schaefer and Harvey Whitehill. He imagined killing them, making them suffer as they died. They had wronged him, and they should pay a price.

He imagined Bill Antrim receiving the punishment he was due for being a no good son-of-a-bitch, a man who cheated women and children. Bill should be the one who ended up broke and alone, freezing and starving on the banks of a river going nowhere. Instead, Bill was sleeping in a cabin next to a fire while his stepson lay on the ground, cold and wet, next to the banks of that no-account river. How were such fates decided? Was this justice?

Henry saw no other people on his way to Globe City, and he spent his days walking along the Gila consumed by his loneliness. His mother was gone. He had no one to care for and no one to care for him. Silver City was becoming a faint memory, and he needed to begin his life anew. He had once thought he would always stand on a platform made strong by the wisdom his mother had given him, but he no longer knew if that was possible. Having never intended to betray her wise advice, he was beginning to see the necessity of amending her gilded proverbs to fit his situation.

If he could make an honest wage, he would. If not, he would have to take what he needed rather than starve. He would treat others with good humor and respect. If they didn't treat him the same, he would protect himself and provide his own justice. He had learned that he could not trust some people, and he always needed to be on guard against the ill will of others. He needed to lay the wood to anyone who might do him harm before they had a chance to harm him.

By the time he arrived in Globe City he would be ready to do whatever it took — legal or illegal — to keep himself alive and free.

August 1877

— 65 —

Almost two years after Henry left Silver City he walked into Atkins' Cantina near Camp Grant in the Arizona Territory looking for a game of faro. The commander-in-charge at Camp Grant had issued a warrant for his arrest, but he was unconcerned. He was cocksure the army's constables would never be able to catch him, and if they did, they would never be able to keep him locked up. He had already shown authorities in two territories that they could not keep him in jail.

Everyone in the Camp Grant area knew him as Kid Antrim. When he had first arrived in Globe City he introduced himself as Henry Antrim because he thought the name McCarty might reveal to others that he was wanted for stealing and breaking out of jail in Silver City. After he got a job at the Sierra Bonita ranch, the cowboys began calling him "Kid," and the name stuck. "He's too small to do a man's work," one of the ranch hands had said.

By the time he walked into Atkins' Cantina on a hot Friday night in August he had come to accept his new name. He was Kid Antrim, vagabond outlaw, wanted by the United States Army for stealing horses, saddles, blankets, and any other items that might fetch money in Tucson. If his outlaw reputation ever caused his stepfather — probably the only other Antrim in Arizona — some discomfort, so much the better.

Henry strutted through the cantina, confident that its patrons would see he was the type of man who would accept their good humor but not their hostility. Although he was still small for his seventeen years, he had learned to carry himself in a way that showed others he was no longer a boy. His clothes, new and unsoiled, would keep others from thinking of him as nothing more than a saddle tramp. His square-toed boots, store-bought wool pants, and blue shirt protected by a stiff leather vest were topped off by a sombrero made distinctive by the embroidered turquoise and gold band circling its crown.

He had acquired the clothes by cheating an honest man named Sorghum Smith. Sorghum had been good enough to give him a job at a hay camp, and after his first day on the job, Sorghum had asked him if he needed an advance on his pay. When Sorghum offered him ten dollars, he asked for forty, saying he needed to buy a few necessities. He then took the forty and left the hay camp, never completing another day of work for the man who had been so generous.

Sorghum's money had not only bought him a new set of clothes, it had allowed him to buy a new gun and throw away the piece of shit he had stolen from his stepfather. He carried his new .45 Colt revolver in a belt and scabbard he had also bought with Sorghum's money. He had stocked up on cartridges for the revolver. He had learned that a good gun and plenty of ammunition were essential to his survival. He had spent hours practicing with the gun and had learned to draw it from its holster without a second of hesitation. He could hit any target within the gun's range, whether he was standing still or on the move.

After first coming to Arizona, he had spent several months looking for work, moving from farm to ranch to mining camp. In most cases he was unable to convince the bosses he was strong enough to do the work. The few ranchers who did take a chance on hiring him usually didn't keep him around long. He hated admitting it to himself, but those who wouldn't hire him were right. No matter how hard he tried he just couldn't do some of the work that the stronger, older, and more experienced ranch hands found so easy.

With no way to support himself and nowhere to go, he had spent countless nights alone in the Sonoran desert, figuring he would never live to see his sixteenth birthday. The freezing night air, the acute hunger, the desperation, all had worked to change his thinking about what it took to be a good man. He had decided that a good man was one who stayed alive — no more, no less. If he could survive by living on the side of the angels, as his mother would have wanted, so much the better — but first he had to survive. And not until a man named Miles Wood fired him from a job at the Hotel de Luna did his fortune change, and he learned how to do more than just survive.

Miles was a thickset man, a Canadian who sported a drooping horseshoe mustache. Miles was intimidating to those who didn't know him well, a bastard to those who did. He had offered Henry a job at the hotel as a cook, offering to pay him fifty cents a day plus room and board. With few cooking skills, Henry accepted the offer, only to fail again at a job that might have provided him a warm place to sleep and something to eat. The large number of soldiers coming to the hotel every evening proved too much for Henry to handle. He couldn't keep such a large number of people fed, and

Catherine's Son

Miles wasted little time telling him he needed to find another job.

But even before Miles fired him, Henry had begun to learn that he didn't need the skills of cooking, ranching, or mining to make a living. The rustlers he befriended at the Hotel had taught him about an easier and more profitable way of making money.

One of the rustlers, a man named John Mackie, had treated Henry with respect and good humor. The man that Henry learned to call Mack was a lean but strong man from Scotland with thick black hair, a well-groomed beard, and a no-nonsense disposition. He was at least a decade older than Henry and a foot taller. He had told Henry that he once made a living as a trumpet player with the Sixth Cavalry at Camp Grant. He also told Henry that he had been discharged for killing a man. He claimed self-defense, and a jury acquitted him, but the Army still discharged him for insubordination. Mack said it was a fair charge. He hated the goddamned Army and didn't care a whit about following their orders.

Mack showed Henry a new way to make money and avoid the menial jobs that paid so little, the jobs Henry often couldn't even do.

"You help me and I'll help you," Mack had said to Henry one night at the Hotel de Luna.

Mack trained Henry in the art of stealing horses, showing him the tricks of the trade and the easy money the thievery could produce. Henry, who had never made much more than a dollar a day working in a saloon, discovered that a single saddle could fetch thirty dollars in Tucson and a horse could bring five times that amount.

Henry was well aware that horse thieves lived in fear of a lynch

218

mob's rope. He knew that men valued their horses above all other possessions. "Horse first, rifle second, dog third, and wife fourth," he had heard others say. Nevertheless, he figured the money was good and Mack was a skilled mentor. Henry could find no one better than John Mackie to show him how to do the work and how to avoid getting caught.

The thievery didn't even challenge his sense of right and wrong. He was mostly stealing from the United States Army, and after hearing everything Mack had told him about the Army, he had no qualms about taking their property. Mack had told him the Army couldn't even protect the Indian women and children massacred at Camp Grant. As far as Henry was concerned, the Army didn't deserve anyone's respect. To hell with them, Henry thought. It was no great crime to steal a few horses from an organization that let ruffians kill women and children.

Henry tried not to steal from those who didn't deserve it. Except for feeling guilty about the forty dollars he stole from Sorghum Smith, he had done little that would bother his conscience. And he had no doubts that he would someday repay Sorghum. He had already returned five horses after finding out they were stolen from a farmer who had depended on the animals to make a living.

With Mack's help, Henry had discovered that he possessed a talent for staying one step ahead of the law. In the few cases when he had been caught, he proved that no one could keep him locked up. Whether he escaped by throwing salt in a guard's eyes or squeezing through a vent in a guardhouse, he never stayed long in a jail cell. He also had no trouble recruiting someone to break his shackles or give him a place to hide. He may have been an outlaw, but he was discovering that even outlaws could find people to give them a hand.

He had traveled a long road searching for what he could do well, and his search had come to an end. He could steal, and he could keep himself free. He was good at those two things, and he knew it.

He even had a long-term plan for abandoning his life as an outlaw. Whether the game was faro or poker, he had learned that he possessed a natural ability to count cards and assess the odds against winning an honest game — and he knew how to avoid the dishonest ones. His youthful appearance made seasoned gamblers think he was easy prey, but they soon learned otherwise. As long as he stayed away from the whiskey and kept his wits about him, no one could cheat him.

And that's what brought Henry to Atkins' Cantina one August night — he was looking for a card game. He walked into the cantina that evening as nothing more than a horse thief looking for an honest game of faro, a proud young man who had learned how to survive in a lawless territory.

— 66 —

"Do you remember me?" asked the man sitting alone at a table in the far corner of the cantina.

Henry had just sat down at a faro table when he looked up to see who was talking to him. The man was older than Henry but didn't look like he'd be much taller when he stood up. He also had a massive chest and seemed to carry more muscle than usual for a man of his height. An empty bottle of whiskey sat on the table in front of him.

"I said, do you remember me? You goddamn runty horse thief."

Henry knew the man. His name was Windy Cahill. He was the guard who had clamped iron shackles on Henry's arms and ankles at the Camp Grant jail. Henry had watched Cahill abuse every prisoner under his charge in that jail. "Windy" was a good name for the son-of-a-bitch because he never shut up. Why no one had yet killed him, Henry didn't know.

"Goddammit, do you remember me?" Cahill said. His words bellowed through the saloon, causing heads to turn and people to stop whatever they were doing. Cahill stood up and walked toward Henry's table.

Henry set his cards down, looked up, and smiled. "Of course, I remember you. How are you doing, Windy?"

"My name's Frank. I have no use for anyone who calls me Windy." Cahill was drunk. He also seemed to be looking for a fight, a fight Henry wanted to avoid.

"I'll call you whatever you want," Henry said. "I'm not looking for trouble."

"You're the little piece of shit that embarrassed me."

"What'd I do?" Henry asked.

"You slid through that goddamned ventilator and escaped from the cell I was guarding. I almost lost my job because of you."

"Didn't mean you no harm, Frank. Just trying to take care of myself."

Cahill had beaten Henry with an old board at the Camp Grant guardhouse. On two occasions Henry had been thrown to the ground and pinned down as Cahill sat on his chest and hit his face with clenched fists. Henry was too small to fight back and was left with no choice other than suffering through the assaults before escaping from the jailhouse at his first opportunity.

"I figure there's a price on your head, and I plan to collect it," Cahill said, standing next to Henry who was still seated and looking up at Cahill.

"You got it wrong. There's no price on my head." Henry was telling the truth. The commander-in-charge had issued a warrant for Henry's arrest, but no reward had been offered. "I'm worth nothing to you, and you might as well get back to your redeye," Henry said.

Henry pushed his chair back and stood up, figuring it was time to walk away from his game of faro and leave the cantina. Before he could back away from the table Cahill shoved both his hands into Henry's chest. Henry lost his balance and fell to the floor, picking himself up only to be shoved again.

"You're nothing but a little girl," Cahill said, pushing Henry toward the center of the cantina. "That goddamned pretty face of yours makes me wonder whether you can even grow a whisker."

Henry had dealt with Cahill's type before. He had learned to simply smile and wait for an opportunity when he had an advantage.

"Those clothes and that hat make you look like a sissified pimp," Cahill said.

"Do you even know what a pimp is?" Henry asked, laughing.

Cahill put his arms on Henry's shoulders and then kicked his feet out from under him. "I said you were a sissified pimp," Cahill said, as Henry hit the floor.

Henry pulled himself up again, realizing Cahill was not going to let him leave the cantina without a fight. He had few options other than trying to catch Cahill by surprise.

Lunging forward, Henry wrapped his arms around Cahill's chest. With little effort Cahill raised his arms, broke Henry's grasp, and shoved Henry again, causing him to bounce off the back of a chair before hitting the floor.

"I've had enough, you pie-eyed son-of-bitch," Henry said, pulling himself off the floor and putting his hand on his gun. Cahill had no weapon of his own and grabbed Henry's arm before he could pull the gun out of its holster. Cahill then twisted Henry's arm behind his back as he pushed him through the cantina's batwing doors and onto the dusty street outside.

"Shit, Frank, I'm not looking for trouble." Pain shot through Henry's entire body as Cahill jerked up on his right arm.

"You embarrassed me at the guardhouse, and you called me a son-of-a-bitch." Cahill shoved Henry to the ground, sat on his chest, and used his knees to pin both of Henry's arms to the ground. Cahill then punched Henry's face repeatedly as Henry remained motionless in the dirt.

"Let me up," Henry pleaded, feeling desperate to break loose. "You're hurting me. Let me up."

As Henry continued taking punishing blows to his head, he pulled his right arm from under Cahill's knee. He then placed his hand on the Colt revolver that was still in its holster and pulled the gun out. He fired a single shot into Cahill's stomach. Cahill slumped to his right, allowing Henry enough room to squirm free.

Henry put the gun back in its holster and pulled himself off the ground. A small crowd had gathered around him. Without saying a word he straightened his sombrero and then ran to a hitching post no more than ten feet away, untying the first horse in line. He then jumped onto the saddle and rode out of town. No one in the crowd tried to interfere with his escape. Maybe they thought Cahill had it coming. Maybe they were afraid that Henry might kill someone else.

Henry rode fast enough to get away from anyone chasing him, but not too fast to wear his horse down. He would need to travel far if he wanted to stay out of jail, and he knew enough to keep the horse fresh. When he sensed that no one was following him he slowed the horse down, even stopping several times to give the animal a rest. If he had been followed out of Camp Grant, he never knew about it.

— 67 —

Henry rode east, heading away from Camp Grant toward New Mexico Territory. Before reaching New Mexico he spent three days camped in the desert outside of Clifton, keeping himself fed for a time with dried beef from the saddlebags on his stolen horse. He had no mirror to see his reflection, but he assumed his face was covered with bruises from Cahill's assault. It certainly felt sore and swollen.

Sitting alone in the desert nursing his wounds, he gave much thought to where he would go next. He couldn't stay in Arizona where he was wanted for murder, and he couldn't return to Silver City where he might end up back in jail. If he kept riding east and stayed away from Silver City, he could look for work somewhere in eastern New Mexico or even Texas. He thought about going south to Old Mexico. Wherever he went, he first needed something to eat, something more substantial than the desert mice and beetles he had been eating after he finished the jerky from the saddlebags. He decided to travel into Clifton for a meal, and if he ran into Bill Antrim, so be it. He'd ignore the old fool like he was just another unwashed digger.

Henry found a saloon on the eastern edge of Clifton, and as he sat in the saloon eating a bowl of stew, a man walked up to him. The man was much older than Henry, probably older than Bill Antrim. He wore a pressed suit that gave him an air of authority. Henry figured he must be a professional man. Maybe an attorney or newspaper reporter. Maybe a gambler.

"You're Kid Antrim," the man said.

"I don't know what you're talking about." Henry placed his right hand on the gun strapped to his belt, the same gun he had used to kill Windy Cahill.

"I was at Atkins' Cantina when you shot that loud mouthed son-of-a-bitch three days ago. The government sends me this way to negotiate beef contracts for the United States Army, and I've seen my share of miscreant behavior in the saloons of this territory. I'm not the sharpest knife in the kitchen, but I'm smart enough to know how to bear witness to a killing. There's no need lying to me, and there's no need to use that gun on me."

"If you're having any thoughts about turning me in, I wouldn't think twice about shooting you," Henry said.

"There's no need to worry. Appears to me the fella you shot had it coming. If you hadn't pulled the trigger, you'd be lying in a box right now instead of him."

"Are you telling me he died?"

"He took his last breath just a few hours after you shot him. It took the coroner's panel less than ten minutes to rule that you should be charged with murder."

"They didn't see it as self-defense?"

"No. You killed an unarmed man, and you didn't do yourself any favors by running off."

"I had no choice. I always get short straw when it comes to the law's accusations."

"That may be, but it's not too late to start over. Looks to me like you should get out of this territory."

The man pulled a quarter eagle out of a pocket on the side of his coat. "Use this to keep yourself fed while you're finding an honest way to make a living. I saw what happened at that cantina, and the way I figure it, you were justified in what you did. Get yourself out of Arizona and start a new life. Looks to me that you're still young enough to put all this behind you. This money should get you started, and you don't need to think about paying me back."

"Why the charity?" Henry asked, suspicious of anyone who would give him money without wanting something in return.

"I watched you do everything you could to avoid fighting that fella at Camp Grant. He kept pushing you and gave you no choice but to defend yourself. I'm also sensing there's some good in you. You remind me of my own son. You look younger than him, but he's a little fella just like you, and if he ever got himself into trouble, I'd hope someone would help him out. You're young enough that you still have a chance to create a good life for yourself. Besides, in the end, you're no more than some mother's child and you deserve a second chance."

The man's good will confounded Henry. After all he'd done living on the wrong side of the law, he doubted he would ever again meet an honest man standing on his side in a controversy. He didn't know the man's name, but he could not have been more grateful for the help. He took the coin, placed it in a pocket on his shirt, and shook the man's hand.

"You can trust I'll use this opportunity well," he told the man.

After finishing his meal and leaving the saloon, Henry climbed on his horse and left Clifton. He had decided to return to New Mexico and ride east toward the Pecos River. It was as good a location as any, he figured.

He had also decided to change his name. People knew Henry McCarty as a thief and fugitive from a Silver City jail. They knew Henry Antrim as a thief and killer in Arizona. He would drop both names and reclaim the identity his stepfather had denied him. He would place his mother's maiden name next to the name he had been given at birth.

With hopes that he could set his life on a different path, he rode toward New Mexico Territory with a new identity — William H. Bonney. He would ask people to call him Billy.

.

New Mexico Territory
September 1877

— ◆ —

— 68 —

Billy Bonney arrived at the Nicolai ranch a short time after the sun came up. A Mexican ranch hand near the Carlisle mines had told him an outbreak of smallpox had caused people to leave Silver City. Billy was told his brother had fled to the Nicolai ranch near Georgetown. Billy hadn't seen Josie in two years and had decided to ride to the ranch and find him. At the very least, he wanted to see someone who could talk about his mother, someone who could tell stories about the good times before she passed away.

As he approached the ranch, he rode toward the stables behind the main house. Through an open barn door he spotted a young man sitting on a stool and preparing to milk a cow. He thought the young man looked like his brother. If so, Josie must have grown a foot and gained thirty pounds. Someone who looked like Chauncey Truesdell stood next to the young man on the stool. If it was Chauncey, he also looked taller and heavier.

Billy climbed off his horse and walked toward the barn. As he got closer, he could see that the two young men were indeed Josie and Chauncey. When Billy's foot snapped an old board lying on the ground, Chauncey jumped and reached for a rifle leaning against the wall. Josie stood up and turned around, knocking his stool over.

"Who's there?" Josie said.

"Don't you know your own brother?" Billy lifted his arms up and away from the gun strapped to his hip. Chauncey was holding a rifle, and Billy didn't want anyone with a gun thinking he was an unfriendly intruder. "There's no need to shoot a friend," Billy said, looking at Chauncey.

"Henry!" Josie said. "I thought I'd never see you again."

Billy hadn't seen such enthusiasm in Josie since the night they stayed up late telling their mother about the circus. Josie's voice had changed, becoming much deeper, almost a man's voice.

Billy shook Josie's hand, then Chauncey's.

"It's great to see you boys," Billy said. He couldn't remember the last time he had felt such a big smile on his own face.

"Look at your clothes, and look at that fancy sombrero," Chauncey said. His voice was also deeper than Billy remembered. "You've become quite the dandy since you left Silver City."

"Just trying not to look like the vagabond I am," Billy said. "Is it true about the smallpox in Silver City?"

"A few people have gotten sick, but most are okay," Chauncey said. "Some left town, but most stayed. My mama stayed to take care of those who did get sick."

"Your mother's a good woman," Billy said. "I guess it's just a rumor, but I was told the town is empty."

"That's an exaggeration," Chauncey said. "I bet no more than a couple dozen people left. Me and Josie would still be there except that Mr. Nicolai hired us to harvest apples and do a few other chores. It wasn't the illness that made us leave."

Josie reached out again to shake his brother's hand. "It sure is good to see you," Josie said. "I heard you had gone to Old Mexico."

"Not true," Billy said. "I've spent the last couple of years in Arizona."

"Are you coming back to Silver City?" Josie asked.

"That depends. Is Mr. Whitehill still sheriff?"

"I'm afraid so."

"In that case I better stay away. I owe that man some jail time, and he'd certainly want me to pay him what I owe him. Besides, I have no desire to return to the reputation I had in that town."

"Where will you be living?" Josie asked.

"I hooked up with some men at Apache Tejo. We'll be taking same cattle to Mesilla."

"You wouldn't be working with Jesse Evans, would you?" Chauncey asked.

"Would anything be wrong with that?"

"Evans is nothing but trouble," Josie said. "He and his boys are rustlers and killers. You should stay away from them."

"You're the only one in our family that ever needed advice," Billy said, laughing at his brother's warning. "I can take care of myself."

"Just thought I'd let you know," Josie said, displaying the familiar hangdog look that Billy had seen often when they were growing up.

"Are you still working for that scar-faced Joe Dyer?" Billy asked Josie.

"He told me to leave the Orleans Club after you escaped from jail. He said he couldn't trust anyone from our family. I didn't mind leaving because I never liked working at his place anyway. I'm living at the Truesdells' now, sleeping in your old bed and working your old job at the Exchange."

"I hope you're not also using my reputation. Has anyone accused you of being a thief?"

"Not yet," Josie said, laughing. "But I have been told I'm lazy, and I'll admit guilt to that accusation. I'm more suited to running numbers than serving food and drinks."

Billy was surprised that Josie's laughter sounded somewhat like his mother's.

"Josie's not the worker you were," Chauncey added. "That's for sure."

"I met a Mexican who told me you'd be at this ranch," Billy said to Josie. "How'd that fellow know you were here?"

"I'm not sure who you talked to, but I spent time living on the Hill after Mr. Dyer put me out. I got to know most of the Mexicans up there before the Truesdells took me in."

"Your family's been good to us," Billy said to Chauncey. "The McCarty brothers can never thank you enough."

"I should tell you that I'm an Antrim these days, not a McCarty," Josie said.

"Why would you take the name of that bastard?" Billy asked. "I had no choice but taking that name in Arizona, but would never take it voluntarily."

"The Dyers were calling me Antrim when I moved in with them, and now everyone in town knows me by that name. It's too late to change, I suppose."

"I'm not sure I want to claim a brother named Antrim."

Josie looked hurt and didn't respond.

"Are you still calling yourself Henry?" Chauncey asked. "I know you never liked that name."

"Mam named me Billy when I was born, and I'm going to reclaim that name. I've decided to call myself Billy Bonney instead of Billy McCarty."

"Why's that?" Chauncey asked.

"I'll be riding east toward the Pecos soon, and when I get there I want a new identity. I want to start over with a name that has no history."

Billy decided not to tell Chauncey the actual reason he needed a new identity. Chauncey came from a good family and was not the type of boy who would associate with a horse thief and killer. Billy was not the same person as when he lived in Silver City, and he wondered whether he would ever again be the type of person who could be friends with someone as honest as Chauncey. He figured that not even Chauncey's parents would support him any more, and Harvey Whitehill would now have a legitimate reason to lock him up and send him to prison.

"Do you mind if I talk with my brother alone?" Billy asked Chauncey.

"Not at all," Chauncey said. "I'll finish milking the cow."

Billy reached into his vest pocket and pulled out a quarter eagle. "Give this to your mama," he said, handing the coin to Chauncey. "I owe her this for helping me get out of Silver City."

"She doesn't want that back," Chauncey said.

"Probably so," Billy said, "but I'd feel better if she took it."

"I'll get it to her," Chauncey said, taking the coin. "You always were more honest that the rest of us."

"Don't let it fool you," Billy said. "I've got enough dishonesty in me to go around.

Billy turned away from Chauncey and left the barn with Josie following behind. The two brothers walked up the valley heading east, away from the ranch. Billy's horse followed them, the reins of its bridle in Billy's hands.

"It was three years ago tomorrow that Mam died," Billy said. "I can't believe it's been that long."

"I don't think about her much," Josie said. "I'm sure you miss her more than me. You were her favorite."

"She loved us both," Billy said, surprised that his brother would say such a thing.

"I don't think that's true."

"Of course it is. She was a good Mam and worked hard for both of us."

"I just don't think about her much."

"Damn it, Josie! She deserves better than that. She deserves to be remembered, especially by her two boys."

"You're the one she cared about, not me. I'll just get by on my own without thinking about her."

"Didn't you learn anything from her?"

"Not like you," Josie said. "You're the one that everyone likes. You're the one that makes people laugh. You learned everything Mam ever told you about being a good man. Whenever somebody calls you a thief, I know it's not true. You'd never do anything wrong because Mam wouldn't allow it. I'm no thief either, but I'll never amount to much like you will."

"You're making too much of this," Billy said. "You're fourteen now, the same age I was when Mam died. When you're my age you'll be on a better path than I've taken."

"I doubt it. I'm sure I'll be reading about you in the papers someday. I'd bet that you'll be an attorney or politician, probably own a good business. Maybe you'll be a sheriff. All I know is that you'll be putting your name on something important. I'll never be anything more than an Antrim."

"The last time I saw you was in that opium den," Billy said, "but look at you now. You're living with the Truesdells. You're working at a good job. I'd say you've done better than me since I left town."

"What have you been doing?" Josie asked.

"Let's just say I've been shit on, hit, and hurt. I'd advise you to do whatever it takes to never go hungry and never engage in killing."

"Have you killed a man?"

"He had it coming. If I hadn't killed him, he might have killed me."

"I can't believe Mam raised a killer," Josie said, shaking his head. "That will follow you wherever you go."

"Trust me, it doesn't feel good to kill a man. But I'll do it again if I have to."

"Mam wouldn't like hearing you talk like that."

"I've had to take a new name because of the man I killed, and I'm hoping to keep the new name unsoiled. I'm hope I never have to kill anyone again. They're still calling me Henry at Apache Tejo, but when I get to the Pecos all that will change."

"I just hope you're not riding with the Evans gang," Josie said. "They've been causing the worse kind of mischief. They're on the wrong side of the law, and you're surely going to end up in a jail cell if you ride with them."

Billy didn't need any reprimands from his own brother and was beginning to wonder why he had ever wanted to see him. What he had hoped to gain by talking with Josie, he didn't know. He certainly wasn't talking about the good times when his mother was alive, as he had hoped. Too much had changed, he figured.

Billy had been living on the wrong side of the law for almost two years and had made a habit of hiding from the authorities. He had "thief" and "killer" stamped on his reputation. And, as Josie suspected, he had joined the Evans gang, a group of rustlers who deserved every bit of their murderous reputation. Billy was an outlaw, plain and simple.

Josie, on the other hand, was living with a good family and earning an honest wage. He seemed to be growing into a good man, someone who would never see the wrong side of the law unless he was standing next to his own brother.

Billy hoped to change his ways when he got to the Pecos. He'd find honest work, marry a good-looking señorita and start a business. When that day came, he'd pay his brother another visit, and maybe then they'd have something to talk about. Until that day, Billy figured he best not spend time stirring up his past. He was no longer the boy he had been in Silver City, the boy his mother wanted him to be. With his mother gone, he now had nothing in common with his own brother, and he never wanted to see his stepfather again. He was on his own.

"I wish you the best," Billy said, shaking Josie's hand. "Maybe we'll have more to talk about the next time I come this way."

"I hope you come back soon."

"We'll see," Billy said.

Billy climbed on his horse and rode away from the Nicolai ranch. He planned to finish his business with the Evans gang at Apache Tejo and then head east to build a better life for himself, a life in which he hoped to make himself worthy of being Catherine McCarty's son.

But first, he had one more stop to make.

— 69 —

It was a warm September night that Abelardo Cisneros sat alone on the Mexican side of Silver City's graveyard. Abelardo lived alone on Chihuahua Hill, and whenever it wasn't raining he walked across town to the cemetery to visit his wife's grave. Sometimes he slept next to her tombstone through the entire night, reluctant to leave her alone and return to town. He had not yet gone to sleep on the night that the boy in the turquoise and gold sombrero came to the cemetery. He would have never seen the boy had the moon not been full and bright.

Abelardo stood far enough from where the boy climbed off his horse that he doubted the boy would see him. His wife's tombstone sat underneath a cottonwood, and the boy would never know he was nearby as long as he remained motionless, standing behind the tree.

Abelardo did not know the identity of the boy, although the small frame of the boy's body looked familiar. The boy took the sombrero off his head and looked down at the wooden marker in front of him. Abelardo then heard the boy reading the words on the marker, his hushed tone carrying strong and clear through the night air.

"In Memory of Mrs. Katherine Antrim, 1829-1874," the boy said. "I wish someone would change the name on your marker."

The old man saw no one else in the graveyard and assumed the boy was talking to the ghost of someone long gone.

"They've spelled your name wrong," the boy continued, "and they've scarred your good reputation with that son-of-a-bitch's last name. You're my Mam and you deserve better."

The boy then turned to look at a tombstone sitting a few feet behind him.

"At least they have Sarah's name spelled right. That may be the only thing anyone in this town ever got right."

Abelardo remained still as he watched the boy turn back around and fall to his knees, facing the marker in front of him. It was a long minute before the boy spoke again. This time his voice was choked with emotion.

"I just wanted you to know how much I loved you," he said. "I miss watching you dance and hearing you laugh. I miss hearing the advice you used to give me, and I want you to know that I learned everything you taught me. I know to avoid hard liquor and not let others force me to do the things I shouldn't do. I know to stand up for those who can't stand up for themselves. I know I should try to live on the side of the angels. I know all of that, even though I've moved away from a few of those things lately. Trust me. I'll soon be back on the right path. When I am, I'll think about how you helped me get there."

The boy stood up and bowed his head. It was several minutes before he spoke again.

"You used to tell me about how they hanged that colored man in New York, and I told you I didn't remember. I wasn't telling the truth. I did remember. I just thought you were better off not knowing how much it troubled me. It still does. I wish I'd told you that I remembered it. I wish I'd thanked you for getting me and Josie out of that city. I was only a little fellow when we lived there, but the things I saw used to scare me."

The boy looked around the graveyard as if he suspected someone might be listening to him. He looked nervous. The old man remained motionless, hoping the boy would not see him.

Again, the boy spoke to the wooden marker at his feet. "I wish I could tell you that I've done well since you passed away, but I haven't made a good showing for myself. If I don't change my ways, I'm going to end up just like that colored man, hanging from the end of a rope."

The boy turned to look over his left shoulder as if he had heard someone else in the graveyard. Abelardo feared that if he breathed too deeply, he would be noticed.

The boy saw no one behind him and turned back toward the marker.

"I was thinking about that laundry you ran in Wichita. I remember feeding dirty linens through those rollers while you turned the crank. The steam was so hot I almost couldn't breathe. I can only imagine how bad it must have been for you and the problems you had with that bloody dog.

"I've been thinking about that laundry lately, and I've decided that what I did for you in that place is what I'm going to do for you now. I'm going to run the dirty linen of all the bad things I've done through some rollers and try to get everything clean. I'm hoping I can use what you taught me to help me turn that crank and make everything right for myself.

"I'm hoping my new name will help keep me out of trouble. I'll be calling myself Billy Bonney." The boy spoke the name as if he was proud of it. "How do you like the sound of that name?"

Abelardo then heard the boy's voice again crack with emotion.

"I wish you were here to call me Billy. I'd love to hear the sound of your voice one more time, especially if you were calling me Billy."

The boy placed his head in his hands. Abelardo listened to the boy weep, washing away his grief with tears of pain.

After the boy regained his composure and wiped the tears from his face, he said goodbye to the marker at his feet. He then put the sombrero on his head and turned to look at the tombstone behind him, the one he had said was marked "Sarah." He tipped his hat to the stone and then climbed onto his horse. He left the graveyard riding east.

As the boy rode away, Abelardo caught sight of him on his horse, silhouetted against the star-filled sky. At that moment, Abelardo recognized the boy as the one he had seen climbing from the jailhouse chimney, the same boy he had watched dancing with a señorita at La Sala on the Hill.

Abelardo remembered talking to the boy at the cantina. He remembered hearing others say the boy was a thief. But that didn't matter to Abelardo. He liked the boy. Whether the boy was a thief made no difference.

"If you've been stealing from those American *pendejos*, you've only been giving them what they deserve," he had told the boy at La Sala.

Abelardo quietly wished the boy well as he watched him ride away. No matter what others might say about that boy, Abelardo would say that his mother had raised him well.

New Mexico Territory
October 1877 – July 1881

Epilogue

Sometime during the fall of 1877, seventeen-year-old Billy Bonney quit the Jesse Evans gang and moved to the town of Seven Rivers in the eastern part of New Mexico Territory. After only a short time in the Seven Rivers area, Billy rode north to the town of Lincoln to take honest work as a ranch hand with John Tunstall, a young and idealistic businessman from England for whom Billy had much admiration and respect.

In working for Tunstall, Billy found himself in conflict with a corrupt and well-armed organization of businessmen and politicians. An organization known as The House controlled Lincoln County and worked in cahoots with the Santa Fe Ring, which controlled the entire New Mexico Territory. By establishing a ranch and mercantile store in Lincoln County, John Tunstall had threatened the political and economic dominance of both The House and the Santa Fe Ring, organizations that would stop at nothing to protect their wealth and power.

In February 1878, men working for The House assassinated Tunstall, and Billy was thrust into the middle of a full-scale war between The House and those who hoped to break its control of Lincoln County. Like most of the participants in that war, Billy fought his battles with a gun. Unlike those he was fighting against, those who had garnered political power for their own benefit, Billy was not protected by the hypocrisy of the law. Needing a scapegoat for the violence and lawlessness in Lincoln County, someone who would deflect attention away from the corrupt territorial political system, the Santa Fe Ring began portraying Billy as a cold-hearted thief and murderer. The Ring's newspapers painted Billy as a symbol of everything that was wrong in the New Mexico Territory.

Eventually, as the conflict in Lincoln County was winding down, Billy attempted to redeem himself and sought a pardon for the crimes he had committed during the war. The territorial governor promised Billy amnesty if he turned himself in and testified before a grand jury about crimes he had witnessed. Billy kept his part of the bargain and testified against the powerful interests controlling Lincoln County, testimony that put his own life in jeopardy. Even so, the governor never granted Billy a pardon. Billy was instead prosecuted for murder and sentenced to hang, becoming the only person convicted of a crime for actions taken during the Lincoln County War.

After a daring escape from jail to avoid execution, an escape in which he killed two guards, Billy was hunted by Sheriff Pat Garret for almost three months before Garrett found him and ambushed him in a dark room. Billy was only twenty-one years old when Garrett shot him through the heart.

Through it all, Billy Bonney — known to the newspapers as Billy the Kid during the last months of his life — never lost the charm that nature gave him or abandoned the good humor that helped him survive. While sitting in a jail cell in Santa Fe with his arms and legs shackled, imprisoned by those who wanted him dead, he was described by a newspaper reporter as "taking it easy." In an interview with the same reporter, Billy said, "What's the use of looking on the gloomy side of everything? The laugh's on me this time."

Although hated and feared by a few, Billy the Kid was loved and admired by many, especially the Spanish-speaking people of the territory who called him *El Chivato* and thought of him as *muy simpático*. In his relentless attempt to stay one step ahead of the law, he never failed to find people who supported him, people who would feed him and hide him from the authorities who were trying to kill him, people who found heroism in his fight against organizations that controlled so much wealth and power.

In the end, it might be said that Billy Bonney fought to survive in the only way he knew how, a way that conformed to the rules of the world in which he lived. Doing his best to stay alive, he found himself turning into a ruthless warrior against the powerful and corrupt forces that controlled Lincoln County and the territorial government in Santa Fe. It was a battle he could not win.

Catherine McCarty may have never imagined that her own son would be led so far astray by the injustices of this world. She might also have thought he was on the side of the angels.

www.ingramcontent.com/pod-product-compliance
Lightning Source LLC
Chambersburg PA
CBHW032035240626
47154CB00003B/915